THE ABSTRACT GRIOT

by Troy L. Thompson

Copyright © 2006 by Troy L. Thompson

ISBN 0-7414-3087-8

Published by:

INFI∞ITY
PUBLISHING.COM

1094 New DeHaven Street, Suite 100
West Conshohocken, PA 19428-2713
Info@buybooksontheweb.com
www.buybooksontheweb.com
Toll-free (877) BUY BOOK
Local Phone (610) 941-9999
Fax (610) 941-9959

Printed in the United States of America

Printed on Recycled Paper

Published July 2006

THIS BOOK IS DEDICATED TO MARCIA LYNN,
MORGAN, AND MATTHEW THOMPSON.

I WOULD LIKE TO TAKE THE TIME TO
ACKNOWLEDGE THE FOLLOWING PEOPLE.

GOD
THE THOMPSON FAMILY
THE MATTHEWS FAMILY
THE AMPHIBIANS
DONNA HOWELL
STEVEN JONES
ANDREA
KARIE
TRACY
KIM
OPUS AKOBEN
THE POEMCEES
JOHN LAWSON
JASON LEWIS

THE ABSTRACT GRIOT

"Washington D.C. has a standard of culture among people of color than any other city."

– Paul Laurence Dunbar: 1900

It was as addictive to me
As nicotine to a chain smoker
One gaze and it had me in its clutches for infinity
It drew me in and once I slowly brought it to my lips
The words pure heaven would be an understatement
It's what brings me back over and over again
Each time, each experience better than the first
I refuse to let a substitute replace you as my first
I refuse to trade this feeling I have for you
with any other

This wasn't written by a poet, but by food critic. J. Paul. He wrote this after his first experience with the Hoppin' John and cornbread at the Grand opening of the Abstract Griot in 1962. The combination of good food and good jazz made The Abstract Griot Washington D.C.'s premiere supper club. Abstract Griot is located on the corner of Bohrer and 6th Ave. NW. Inside are tables and booths are along the left wall. On the tables are red and white checkered tablecloths, condiments and fresh flowers. On the hardwood floor are about twenty small circular tables topped with the same items. To the right is the bandstand. Exposed brick walls are filled with black and white framed photos of jazz ancestors such as Duke Ellington, Billie Holiday, Miles Davis and John Coltrane as well as rare concert posters. Towards the back is the kitchen where you can order anything from applesauce to jambalaya. The walls on the second floor are adorned with African masks and artwork by local artists.

The third floor had been transformed into a loft. On Sundays, many members from the Florida Avenue Baptist Church, which is located across the street, come over to enjoy the jazz brunch buffet while listening to the music of the Tucker Mills Quartet. For 15 dollars you can enjoy an all you can eat buffet while your ear feeds on pure jazz music.

When Kenneth "Culture" Baker first opened the Abstract Griot, his original vision was to create an atmosphere where black folks could come together, enjoy good food, good jazz and good company. Culture invested his life savings into the Abstract Griot and ran a successful restaurant for thirty years. He retired in 1992 and sold the business to his son Kenneth Baker Jr. Thirty year old Kenny Jr. had just graduated with an MBA in International Business from Hampton University in Hampton, VA. When he purchased The Abstract Griot, he maintained many of his father's traditions, but Kenny was from the hip-hop generation. He had a vision for The Abstract Griot as well. To attract many of his peers, Kenny dropped the prices on the menu to make them more reasonable for the students from nearby Howard University. He added a freestyle night and a poetry night to attract local talent. Since he had asthma he established a strict no-smoking policy and added some framed graffiti pieces in the art gallery. The Abstract Griot's diverse twenty something crowd complete with locks, baggy pants, slang and attitude. This change sent some jazz purists running to places like HR57, One Step Down and Blues Alley. But those who knew Kenny since he bussed tables and swept the floors as a child understood and applauded his intentions of bringing two cultures together. Kenny felt that he achieved what he wanted. He knew many of his customers on a first name basis and although they were as diverse as the music itself, at The Abstract Griot they were family.

Spring 1997

Paradise

"Voila!" Miss Bessie swiveled the barber chair to the mirror as Evelyn "Paradise" Patterson observed Bessie's latest masterpiece. As Paradise rubbed the close-cropped ringlets all over her head she couldn't hide the wide smile on her face. She concluded that the hour long wait and the hours of work done to her hair were definitely worth it.

"I think they look beautiful," Miss Bessie chimed. "Just wait until your locks grow out girl, they'll really be beautiful."

Paradise got out of the chair and stretched. She reached in her purse for her VISA card and gave it to Miss Bessie, the owner of Au Natural, processed and returned the card to Paradise. Paradise took her card and signed the receipt.

"I recommend that you not shampoo your hair for four weeks but you can rinse your hair and it will stay clean, use this oil on your scalp to prevent flaking." Miss Bessie said.

"Thank you." Paradise smiled as she reached for the oil.

"In four weeks I want you to come and see me child and call if you have any questions."

Paradise placed the red fitted Philadelphia Phillies baseball cap into her backpack and strolled confidently out the door. She finally did it! After two years of debating she finally locked her hair. She was tired of putting chemicals in her hair and for a year had put five different styles of braids in her hair. God only knows how much money that cost her. When she pulled her braids out on Saturday night she knew it was time. She was glad she did it on a Sunday because there was hardly anyone there. Her week's vacation was over so

3

she decided to end Sunday night the best way she knew how, poetry night at The Abstract Griot.

Paradise took the Eastern Market escalator down to the Metro and looked at her watch, poetry night had started. She grabbed her fare card out of her pocket, put the card through the machine and walked through the turnstile. After she transferred from the orange line to the green line train, she arrived at the Shaw/Howard University station. Paradise walked up the street and arrived at her destination, The Abstract Griot. Sunday night poetry lasted from 6p.m. to 9p.m. When Paradise arrived at the door, the clock on the wall said 7:15. Toni, who hosted poetry night, was on stage reciting a poem in her trademark, comfortable, storytelling style. Paradise strolled in and made her way to a table. From the stage, Toni's and Paradise's eyes met, Toni smiled and flashed her a peace sign without disturbing her flow. Paradise returned the peace sign and headed towards the table where she saw her friend Mood dressed in a pair of blue jeans and a black Miles Davis tee shirt.

From his table Mood watched Paradise's 5'7" slender body walk in the door and move through the crowd towards him, he noticed how her new baby locks complimented her cocoa brown skin. When she got to the table he reached over to hug her bony frame.

"What's up Mood?" She whispered.

"It's all about you right now," Mood whispered back. "When did you get these done?" He asked while gently caressing the top of her head.

"Just a few hours ago," she answered. "What do you think?"

"I didn't think you could perfect perfection," He said in his trademark smooth voice. "They really compliment your beauty."

"Thank you." She sat down at the table and turned to the stage. "Have you read yet?" She asked not taking her eyes off the stage.

"No I'm still waiting, Are you gonna read?"

"Yeah, I got this one piece I just wrote." As Toni finished her poem, the whole place erupted into applause. After she introduced Mood, she got off the stage and walked straight to her table where she had a warm dinner waiting. Mood proceeded on stage, thanked Toni and pulled the microphone stand to him, raised it and said to the audience. "Good evening ladies and gentlemen, this piece is entitled:

BREAKFAST IN BED

One evening to cater to your every desire
Making love from night to day
Multiple ecstasies taking us higher
Pleasing each other sexually as we lay

As I enter you, you moan of pleasure
As we rock to the rhythm of motion
A night I will cherish forever
Full of unconditional love and emotion

My body is burning from the heat of passion
As you tongue me all over to cool me down
Calling out your name in satisfaction
Sexually lifting me off the ground

I kiss you from your head to your feet
And I fulfill all of your fantasies
As the sweat of your bodies dampen the sheets
I make sure all of your desires are pleased

The daylight breaks through the window
As I kiss you on the forehead
Thinking of how much I love you as I go
To make you breakfast in bed

After his poem he said, "Thank you." For the applause he received and watched Paradise return from Toni's table.

"I just put my name on the list, I go on after Generation Next."

Soon Toni introduced Paradise. Toni described their first meeting when Paradise was a senior at UDC and their performance at a Black History Month celebration, which Paradise organized for the English Department. After she introduced Paradise, there was applause as Paradise took the stage. She hugged Toni as Toni went to her table and took a seat. Paradise opened her small notebook and said "What's up? I want to share with y'all this piece called:

SUNDAY IN HARLEM (Candice's story)

Looking out my window trying to escape my anger
I light a cigarette to my mouth to clear my mind
I look out to a beautiful sunny day in Harlem
But the sun doesn't shine on my side of the block
I don't hear no birds singing because there are no trees
On my block for pretty birds, just pigeons leaving droppings on the street
So for singing I place Lady Day on the phonograph to hear her sing
I look down at everyone on their way to church
And like every Sunday I tell myself I'm definitely going next week
But I never do and blame it on my broken alarm clock
That works great everyday except on Sundays
Looking down on my stoop I see John's meeting with his bookie
To place a bet on the horse race and Charlie, the building's custodian, who's daydreaming
So hard he doesn't even notice the neighborhood madam eyeing him suggestively
In front of our stoop is the reason for my anger.
My husband Ted

He's smoking a cigarette also to cool of from our
argument
And then go to his mistress' apartment in Coney Island
I found out about her when old Ms. Herman asked me
How did I like my flowers she saw Ted buy for me
I haven't seen flowers from Ted since our wedding day
I found out later he's been seeing his old high school
sweetheart
Who had his child, I always wanted a child
Today I finally confronted him about his affair

After a heated argument he called me a bitch
And storms out the house I throw a plate at him as he
leaves
Lucky for him it missed and shattered when it hit the
floor
So as Lady Day sings God bless the child in the
background
I realize that I am blessed although I don't go to church
I know that God is watching me. So with that in mind
I fling my cigarette into the gutter and start to
Pick up the pieces of my life and the shattered plate
I put on my heels and go to church to pray to the
Only man who hasn't let me down and as I walk out
my house
The sun shines a little brighter on my side of the block.

Thank you.

The people clapped as she left the stage. After poetry
night ended, Kenny came down from his office to greet
Paradise as she left.

"Hey Kenny, I haven't seen you all night." Paradise
said.

"I've been on the speaker phone with my father
working on ideas for our thirty-fifth anniversary celebration.
I'm trying to surprise him by reuniting his old jazz band,

Nomad. Everyone here would go wild to see them together but he's so damn stubborn. Mom said Scat's the only band member he will ever talk to," He paused. "Paradise, your hair really looks nice."

"Thanks," She smiled. "I've been getting some really good vibes on it. I was hoping Flame would be here so she could see them."

"I heard Antigravity had a show in Baltimore or else she'd be here, you know how much she loves poetry and she would have loved "Sunday in Harlem.""

"Did you like it?" Her almond eyes lit up.

"I sure did, I put Dad on hold just to hear it."

"You're brave, your Pops usually don't play that." She said.

"Oh I know, but he can't do anything but yell at the phone." Just then Mood approached them.

"Hey Mood." Kenny greeted.

"What's going on Kenny, the Hoppin' John was the bomb tonight man." Mood said as he gave Kenny a pound.

"Thanks man, I've got to keep you coming back." Kenny said.

Mood then turned to Paradise and asked. "Do you need a ride home?"

"Yes I do. Kenny, I'll check you out soon."

"Okay." He hugged her goodbye and shook Mood's hand.

"Have a good evening and be careful locking up." Mood said as they walked away.

After Mood dropped Paradise off in front of her apartment building, she opened the door and checked the clock, it was 10:15. She was glad Mood offered her a ride home, it would've taken forever on the Metro on a non-rush hour Sunday night. Paradise pulled the plastic off of her freshly dry cleaned pants suit and dreaded going back to work. She changed out of her clothes and put on her satin Victoria's Secret night shirt. She got on her knees to pray, turned on her radio to WSOL's slow jams, turned off her lights and climbed into bed. The music lulled her into a deep sleep.

At 8:30 a.m., Paradise made coffee in the conference room area of the Campbell-Jones Investment Agency. She returned to the front desk of the reception area and placed the newspapers neatly on the high front desk next to the neatly shelved in-box. Greg McGovern, the agency's manager, got off the elevator reading the *Wall Street Journal* and eating an apple. He walked into the office without looking up from his paper.

"Good morning." This was the routine every morning for the three years she worked there.

"Good morning Mr. McGovern." Paradise said.

"Welcome back Evelyn, how was your vacation?" He asked. His smile turned to surprise when he looked at her hair.

"It was fine," Paradise noticed his expression. "I stayed in town and did the tourist thing, visiting museums and going to see art exhibits."

Mr. McGovern, an average sized, skinny brown haired man in glasses said. That's nice." He turned to go into his office. "When Ms. Paul gets in tell her I need to see her in my office."

"Yes sir." A few minutes later Kathy Paul arrived. Ms. Paul is Paradise's supervisor. She was a beautiful blonde in her early forties, she's six feet tall in heels. She had long strong legs from all of her college victories as a member of the Princeton University swim team. As soon as she walked in the door, she dropped her briefcase in front of Paradise's desk.

"Good morning Evelyn, I'm so glad you're back. How was your vacation?"

"It was fine." Paradise smiled.

"Jenny, the temp we had, was a real air head, we have a busy week ahead of us. The owners of the agency are supposed to be here on Wednesday and stay until Friday for a progress meeting, it's supposed to be very important. Maybe one of them will marry me and take me away from Mr. McGovern." She joked.

"Oh yeah," Paradise remembered. "Speaking of Mr. McGovern, he wanted to see you in his office when you arrived."

"He'll see me after I see a cup of coffee." Ms. Paul said. "Jenny couldn't even make a decent cup of coffee, what a shame. By the way, I love your hair."

"Thanks Ms. Paul." Paradise said.

"Now get back to work, you already had your vacation, I better go see what the warden wants." Ms. Paul said as she picked up her briefcase and went to his office.

The morning dragged on as most Monday mornings do, when Paradise looked up at the clock it said 11:15. "At least it's almost lunchtime." She thought as she spent the morning doing the filing that her temp Jenny didn't do. The phone rang as Paradise rolled her chair to the phone.

"Good morning, thank you for calling Campbell-Jones, my name is Evelyn. How may I direct your call?"

"To you girl!" The voice on the other side of the phone said.

"Hey Flame, What's going on?" Paradise was happy to hear from her friend. "How was your show last night?"

"You know how it goes, The sound man was garbage and the crowd was rowdy. What are you doing for lunch?"

"I'm not sure yet, with the mess the temp left behind I may be working through it," Paradise said. "Besides we got some VIP's coming in this week."

"Why don't you come through so you can check out the new Antigravity demo we just put together?"

"Where are you Flame?"

"I'm here at Tower Records working, we can grab lunch from Subway. I want your honest opinion on this."

"I'm on my way, I have something I want you to see

10

too." After Paradise hung up the phone, she got up and stretched then walked down the hall to Ms. Paul's office. Ms. Paul was working on her computer when Paradise knocked on her door.

"I'm on my way to lunch. Can I get you anything from Subway?" "No thanks I have a salad. Evelyn, have a seat please." Paradise looked confused, It was rare that Ms. Paul took a serious tone with her.

"Yes ma'am." She sat down. "Mr. McGovern asked me in his office to discuss you, or should I say your hair. Company policy prohibits extreme or fad hairstyles and while I think he's being a prick, he thinks your hair fall within these guidelines. He asked me to bring this to your attention. I did some research and found the policy on dress codes and it's in there." Ms. Paul hands Paradise a copy of the company policy with the dress code highlighted. It states:

No extreme or fad hairstyles
No facial rings besides earrings (women only) to include nose rings, tongue rings, etc.
Appropriate dress, no tennis shoes, jeans, baseball hats, and shorts.

"I'm sorry my hands are tied here." Ms. Paul said as she saw the pained look on Paradise's face.

"Well, I'm sure you did what you could and I appreciate that." Paradise got up to leave.

"We'll talk more about it later, go ahead to lunch. I'll watch the phones until you return."

Paradise put on her headphones and walked out of the building to the McPherson Square Metro. Tower Records was two Metro stops up. When she arrived at the Foggy Bottom Metro she walked up I Street. When she got to Tower she walked up the stairs to the second floor and found Flame behind the cash register. Flame looked up and saw Paradise coming towards her.

"Oh shit! Your hair is the bomb," She said. "I dig them for real."

"Thanks." Paradise forced a smile from her lips.

"What's wrong? I know it's your first day back at work and all but..."

"I'll tell you in a minute." Paradise said. Flame asked for assistance at her register and a huge black guy with a Fat Albert tee shirt and a pair of camouflage pants arrived.

"Smiley, cover for me. I'm gonna run to lunch with Paradise." Flame picked up her jacket.

"No problem, What's up Paradise?" Smiley asked.

At Subway, the ladies ordered a twelve-inch Turkey sub and split it. Flame sat across from Paradise with her eyes closed, she nodded her head to the beat. Paradise listened to the three-song demo in her walkman. "This is nice, where did you get the sample for song two from?"

"That's from an old Jackson 5 album that FOG had laying around." Flame said. I'm glad Antigravity has a producer in the group Yo!"

"What's wrong? I can tell something's bothering you." Flame asked.

"My job is tripping off of these." Paradise brushed her hand back and forth on her hair. "My supervisor told me they're against company policy, they may ask me to cut them off." She handed Flame a copy of the company's dress code. "I never thought this would jeopardize my job."

"Why don't you call EEOC? It sounds like something they can help you with." Flame encouraged her friend.

"That's a good idea." Paradise sipped on her iced tea. When Paradise returned to work, she looked up the EEOC's number in the phone book and called from the pay phone in the lobby. A secretary took down her phone number and told her someone will be calling her soon. Paradise gave the secretary her work number since she's the only one who answers the phone at work.

Paradise waited for the remainder of the day for someone from the EEOC to call. She didn't leave her desk at all. At 5:00, when she didn't get a phone call she called back and got a prerecorded message. It stated that the E.E.O.C. closed at 4:30 and to leave a message after the tone. She hung up the phone, grabbed her purse and headphones and headed out the front door.

At 8:30, Tuesday morning Mr. McGovern walked in and saw Paradise's hair still twisted in tiny locks.

"Good morning, Mr. McGovern." Paradise faked a smile.

"Good morning Evelyn."

"Your wife wants you to call her, she said it had something to do with her car keys."

"Thank you, I'd better call her," He paused. "How long have you been working here?" Mr. McGovern asked.

"About three years, you hired me right out of college." She forced a smile.

"Oh." He picked up his *Wall Street Journal* from the desk and walked into his office. Ms. Paul walked in with a box of Dunkin Donuts.

"Would you like a jelly doughnut?" She asked.

"Thanks Ms. Paul, this will go perfectly with my milk." Paradise grabbed a jelly doughnut.

"You're welcome." Ms. Paul smiled. "If you need me I'll be in my office working on some last minute details for tomorrow's big meeting. Please take messages for me, if Richard Gere calls tell him I'm ready." Ms. Paul joked.

"Only if he brings Denzel with him." Paradise joked back.

Ms. Paul laughed all the way to her office. Paradise's workday had been normal. She hardly saw Mr. McGovern, he's been on a teleconference with colleagues in New York all day. It was 10:30 when she paged Ms. Paul.

"Ms. Paul, I need to run to the ladies room."

"No problem, I'll watch the phones."

While Paradise was in the ladies room, the phone rang, Ms. Paul picked it up and answered. "Campbell- Jones Investments."

A man's voice said. "May I speak to Evelyn Patterson?"

"She stepped out for a moment, would you like to leave a message?" She asked.

"Yes, Could you tell her Mr. Ernest from the E.E.O.C. returned her call."

"No problem, I'll be sure to let her know." Ms. Paul lied.

That night at The Abstract Griot, Opus Akoben performed on stage. Paradise sat at the bar with a big bowl of jambalaya, a side of cornbread and a cup of hot tea. She wore a brown shirt, a beige pair of cargo pants, boots and a peace sign hanging around her neck. Suddenly from behind, a pair of hands covered her eyes.

"Who's ashy hands are covering my eyes?" She asked.

Raindance from Antigravity removed his hands and sat on the barstool next to hers.

"I knew I should've gotten here earlier, this place is always full when Opus performs. Next time I'm gonna bring my beach chairs." He joked and Paradise laughed.

"I love your dreads! Are you gonna let them grow as long as mine?" Raindance shook his shoulder length locks back and forth.

"Well, it depends on how long I keep them."

"Hold up! One doesn't decide to get locks for a week and then get rid of them."

"I know, I'm having trouble at work. They're saying it's inappropriate and gave me some bullshit dress code policy. I called E.E.O.C. yesterday and I haven't heard anything from them yet."

"Well, I'm not really surprised," Raindance said. "When people see locks in this conservative town, the first thing they assume is that you are a weed smoker. There's a whole history behind locks that people don't even know about." He pointed to his free-flowing locks. "There are even religious reasons why people wear locks. Maybe you should tell them that your locks are spiritually-based."

"I can't, That would be a lie and it would be disrespecting Rastafarians. I won't take advantage of their religion that way. I'll figure something out."

Kenny walked up to them from behind the bar and gave Raindance a pound. "Can I get you anything Raindance?"

"Just an orange juice, I'm on a fruit diet this week."

"Oh for real, hold on." Kenny ran into the kitchen and came out with a huge bowl of grapes and placed them on the bar. "Here you go." He said proudly.

"Wow!" Raindance said. "You know you ain't nothin' but the truth."

"Well I've got to keep you coming back." He said.

After Paradise paid her bill, Kenny asked. "Don't you have a degree in English?"

"Yeah I do."

"Why haven't you used it?" Kenny asked.

"Well, I got this job right out of college and got lazy." Paradise said.

"You should look into that." Kenny said.

"You've worked hard for your degree and you should use it."

"I know, I'll look into that." She said as she rose to leave.

"I hate to eat and run but I've got a very big day tomorrow. The owners of the company are supposed to be in town and stay for a couple of days." She hugged Raindance and Kenny from across the bar.

"Hmmm. Do you think that may have anything to do with it?" Raindance asked.

"Probably, my boss is a big ass kisser." She said as she started to leave.

15

The next morning, Paradise got up and showered. As she dried herself, she looked at her locks in the mirror. She shook her head the way she saw Raindance shake his and she honestly saw the possibility of shoulder length locks and the beauty of them. She went to her bedroom and put on a solid navy blue suit and her shoes and left for work. When Paradise got off the elevator, she walked in the office and was shocked by what she saw. A blond woman sat at her desk.

"Good morning, May I help you?" She asked Paradise.

"You can get up out my seat and away from my desk." Paradise said.

"Are you Evelyn?" She asked. "My name is Jenny, I was here last week. They asked my temp agency if I could work here for a few days," Then Jenny asked. "Why would they want me here if you're here?"

"That's what I'd like to know." Paradise said.

Just then Mr. McGovern came out of his office. "Good morning Evelyn. Can I see you in my office please?"

In the three years that she worked there, the only other time she was in Mr. McGovern's office was during her final interview when she first got the job. "He still has that 80's motif." She thought.

"Mr. McGovern, why is Jenny here working at my desk?"

"Well I needed a few temps while the owners are here. Since Jenny worked the front desk last week, I thought you'd be more effective in the mail room with the other new temps."

Paradise smelled the bullshit. "What did Ms. Paul have to say about this?"

"Actually." Mr. McGovern said as he cleaned his glasses. "It was her idea."

Paradise couldn't believe what she was hearing. "This is bullshit." She thought. "They're gonna stash me in the back and hide me until the owners leave."

"I'm sorry Mr. McGovern." She said with a lump in

16

her throat. "But I cannot let this job dictate the way I'm gonna live my life, I resign." She turned to leave.

As she left his office and proceeded out the front door Ms. Paul entered. She looked at Paradise and then looked down.

"You know you could've told me." Paradise said.

"I know, I tried to get here early enough, I thought it would be less painful coming from me." Ms. Paul said.

Paradise picked up her nameplate from her desk and said. "I bet your knife cuts just as deep." She walked out the office.

When she got home she kicked off her shoes, reached in her backpack for her poetry book and a pencil and began to write poetry. She put all of her anger into her prose. Looking down, she saw the *D.C. City Reader* and thought about what Kenny said. The *D.C. City Reader*, a free Washington weekly newspaper, detailed area events and politics. She flipped it open to page three and copied down the address. She changed into a pair of jeans and a long-sleeved shirt. She grabbed some writing samples from her files and went to the office of the *Reader*.

Mary Grace drank her third cup of coffee, while desperately calling every writer on her roster. She needed to get someone to the Mary McLeod Bethune Council House for its dedication ceremony. It was to become a national historic site managed by the National Park Service. Cicely Tyson is the keynote speaker.

"Excuse me, Are you Mary Grace?" Paradise asked.

"Yeah, I can't talk right now." She said in a New York accent without looking up.

"I understand you're busy, I just wanted to leave my writing samples and this resume' to be considered for employment."

"You're a writer?" She looked up. "Wait, have a seat."

Mary looked over her work and said a silent thank you to God. "Impressive, I like your style. Have you written anything recently?" She asked.

"Not for a publication, but I've been writing consistently." She sat up in her chair.

"Are you busy this afternoon?" Mary asked. "I need a writer to go to the Bethune Council House and cover a dedication ceremony." She handed the press kit to Paradise and asked. "Can you do it?"

"I'm there." She said confidently.

"Good! Go to photos and have Rico hook you up with a press pass."

"YESSSSS." She thought. As she got up to leave Mary said. "Hey Evelyn, I like your hair."

MOOD

At 7:00 a.m. Theodore "Mood" Moody sat in his small work area at the far end of the lobby in the Genesis Building reading the Metro section of the *Washington Post*. The article that caught his eyes was about another senseless death. The story involved a little girl who was in the wrong place at the wrong time, for that she received a bullet in her head. He took off his glasses, rubbed his eyes, and said a prayer for the deceased and her family. He looked at the clock on the wall, it said 7:15. "She should be here any minute." He thought. Mood got up and quickly inspected himself. Mood wore his two piece suit, a white shirt, and a black tie. On his feet, Mood wore a black pair of wingtip shoes. He adjusted his tie and walked up to the front the lobby. There is two glass doors and large windows on either side of the door. While Mood waited, a white Dodge Caravan pulled up to the front of the building. The driver walked around to the sliding door and pulled out a folded wheelchair. After he unfolded the wheelchair, he wheeled it around to the passenger side and helped his wife out of the van and into the wheelchair. He kissed her goodbye and got back into the van and drove away. As she began to wheel herself in, Mood held the glass door open for her.

"Good morning Mrs. Brown."

"How are you Theodore?" She smiled. "You know I can't complain." He said as he pushed the wheelchair to the open elevator and pushed the ninth floor button.

"Thank you, you're such a sweetheart." She smiled.

"You better stop flirting with me or I'm gonna have to take you from your husband." He joked. She laughed as the elevator door closed.

Mood is a six foot tall charismatic brother. He's brown skinned with a shaved bald head, a thin Clark Gable mustache, and glasses. He's been the concierge at the Genesis Building for a year. Pablo, one of the building's three engineers walked in carrying two cups of coffee.

"Good morning Mood man," He said with a mild accent. "I got your coffee."

"Thanks Pablo," Mood handed him two dollars. "How's your family doing?"

"They're doing fine, My little boy is learning his ABC's and he just drew this for me."

He placed the coffee on the counter and pulled a folded drawing out of his uniform pocket. It was a drawing in red crayon of two figures above it read "Me and my Daddy." "I'm going to hang this in my office." Pablo said proudly.

"I bet you he loves his father very much." Mood said.

"Is Mr. Blake here yet?" Pablo asked.

"Not yet." Mood said still standing by the door.

"If he's looking for me I'll be in the tool room, you can reach me on the radio." Pablo said as he pushed the elevator button. The elevator arrived and Pablo got on.

Lydia Tucker, Vice President of Doubleday Temps, walked in the building. Lydia is a thirty seven year old woman who looked twenty five. She had dark brown skin and the sexiest lips on planet earth. As she walked in, Mood grabbed the coffee from the counter and handed it to her.

"Good morning Lydia." Mood smiled. "Hi Theodore, how sweet, thank you." She reached for the cup of coffee.

"Be careful, this coffee is about as hot as you look right now." While she waited for the elevator she put her briefcase on the floor.

"I have a lot of work to do, so much I may have to miss lunch." She eased her foot out of her shoe, curled her toes and placed her foot back in her high heel shoe.

"Well, call me if you need anything for lunch, I'll even massage your feet while you eat to help you relax." Mood said.

"I didn't know your services included foot massages." Lydia smiled.

"It's an exclusive service." Mood said as the elevator door opened.

"I'll definitely let you know." She said as the elevator door closed.

As the morning progressed, the lobby filled with employees. The twelve floor office building has at least 500 employees come through and Mood made every employee feel good about coming to work. George Clark, who worked for Royal Property Management, walked into the building wearing a navy blue suit, a white shirt and a matching navy blue tie. He carried a casual set of clothes on a hanger.

"Good morning George." Mood said reaching to give him a pound.

"How are you today Theodore?" George asked while removing his sunglasses.

"I'm doing alright, It's been a good morning so far. Everything is running smooth, you're the first one from the office to arrive."

"Good. I need a few minutes to wake up before Mr. Blake gets here."

Mood noticed his clothes and asked. "Are you planning on leaving early today?"

"Yeah, we're going to the Washington Bullets game tonight. Royal has a sky box at US Air Arena."

The elevator opened, George entered and asked Mood to "Call the office when Mr. Blake gets in."

"No problem." Mood said who wondered why George still wore a fade.

Ten minutes later Mr. Blake walked in. Mr. Blake is a 5'8 man with a short salt and pepper afro. Mr. Blake's been working with Royal Property Management for over twenty five years. He also owns an apartment building near Georgetown University that he usually rents out to college students. He walks up to Mood's desk with a bag of dirty shirts

"Good morning Theodore, can you get these taken care

of for me? I'm going to need them back by tomorrow morning."

"No problem." Mood said and pulls out a service ticket and fills it out for the shirts. "George is here and Pablo is walking from floor to floor checking the lights."

Mr. Blake saw the open newspaper on the desk. "Theodore! You're here to work, not to read the newspaper."

"Yes sir." He placed the newspaper in his desk drawer.

"Do I have any messages?" "Yes, a Dr. Carver called about the game at the US Air arena. He wants you to call him if anything changes, here's his number." Mood hands him a page from the small message pad.

"Thank you, we're supposed to be leaving at 4:30. Could you make reservations at Georgia Brown's for dinner at 5:00 for a party of eight please?"

"Consider it done." Mood said.

"Thank you." Mr. Blake said. As the elevator opened, he walked on board.

Mood picked up the phone and contacted George.

"He's on his way up."

During the day, Mood worked hard ordering lunch for three different office meetings, picking up dry cleaning, and trying to get last minute tickets to the Bullets game for various clients. Before he knew it, it was noon. At 12:30, Pablo came in with a hot pastrami sandwich with mustard. He thanked Pablo and paid him. At 12:35 Mrs. Brown rolled out the elevator in her wheelchair.

"Hi Theodore, Would you like anything while I'm out?" She asked.

"I've got this for you to save you a trip." He handed her the sandwich.

"Thank you, that's really nice of you."

"Not a problem." Mood smiled.

The mailman walked in and approached Mood from behind. "What's up Mood?"

"Hey what's up Dove?" He gave his friend a pound. "How's the family doing?"

"Everyone's doing fine, Did you hear about tonight?"

"What's happening tonight Dove?"

"The Amphibians are performing and hosting a hip-hop poetry showcase at The Abstract Griot. Participation is on a sign-up basis." Dove unloaded his mail on the freight elevator.

"Are you planning on going?" Mood asked.

"Yeah I'm going, I need to get out of the house and hang out."

"What about you?" "I'm there, I'm working on a piece right now." Mood said.

"Cool, I'll be back down in about twenty minutes." Dove said as the elevator door closed.

The afternoon dragged. Every time Mood looked at his watch he thought time had stopped. He took advantage of the slow afternoon by finishing the poem when he heard a female voice say "Haven't I seen you at The Abstract Griot?"

Mood looked up to see a 5'4' woman with honey brown skin who wore a black DKNY tee shirt with white lettering, a pair of blue jeans, a beige jacket and a black DKNY baseball cap. Her long hair hung out the back in a ponytail.

"Moody Man or something like that."

"Actually, it's Mood, but I'm Theodore Moody here." He stood up and made direct eye contact. "DAMMMN." He thought "She's the bomb!"

"You're the best dressed security guard I've ever seen."

"I'm not a security guard, I'm a concierge." He said.

"What's that?" She asked.

Mood got smooth "A concierge is someone who performs duties for the people of the building so their day can run smoothly. I get tickets, order lunch and perform duties to help the employees of the building have a easier day."

"Oh, so you're a glorified security guard." She joked.

He laughed thinking to himself. "DAMMMN! Beauty and a sense of humor." "Well." He said. "There's a hip-hop poetry event going on at The Abstract Griot tonight. I'll even buy you dinner with my glorified security money."

"I have plans, I'm going to the Bullets game." She said.

"Word, well I hope you have a good time."

"We'll see, I'm going with my father and some people he works with."

Mood started putting things together. "Are you going to eat at Georgia Brown's for dinner?"

"I think so." She walked toward the elevator.

"Have a good time tonight Mood."

"Wait, what's your name?" He asked.

"My name's Sabrina Blake." She said waving goodbye as the elevator door closed.

At 4:30, Mood watched Mr. Blake's entourage leave the building. Sabrina and two others hopped into George's Lexus while Dr. Carver and Mr. Blake hopped into Mr. Blake's Mercedes. They were to meet two others at Georgia Brown's.

Later that night at The Abstract Griot, The Amphibians were on stage performing. Mood sat in a booth with Hawk, Dove, FOG and Dynamite while Paradise took pictures to go with the interview that she did with the Amphibians for the *D.C. City Reader*. Flame and Dana were chillin' at the bar checking out the show. Everyone was taking advantage of the all you can eat buffet that Kenny had prepared and sold for $2.99. After the Amphibians' set was over, Raindance arrived right on time for Antigravity to take the stage. Accompanied by a live band, Antigravity performed one of their old cuts "Transgressions." and a new song called "Melancholy Blues." FOG grabbed the mic and beat boxxed while Flame, Dynamite and Raindance freestyled. The crowd loved it. When they got off stage, heads gave them love. Hawk and Dove performed next. They entered the stage dressed in old Adidas sweat suits and shelltoe Adidas with fat laces. They performed the first song "Classic Hip-Hop." where they briefly broke down the history of hip-hop music. This warmed the crowd up for their new song "Thank You for Your Patience." a song which thanked the real hip-hop heads for keepin' it real and telling everyone to hold on because real hip-hop will soon dominate again as it did before. Mood was next. He got on stage and took the microphone off the stand. Then sat on the edge of the stage, looked directly into the eyes of a girl sitting across from him, cued the bass player, and began his poem.

Orally, I enter
Hands pressed gently on your inner thigh
As my tongue explores
The inner regions of your soul
Many brothers tell you you're so fine
They'll drink your bath water
I'm here to say you're so beautiful
That I will gladly drink your sweet nectar
You're so beautiful, I'd want to grow angelic wings
And fly you around the starry lit sky
Paint your toenails my favorite color
And make love to you like it's a righteous ritual
And after you've reached your climax
I want to hold your warm body close to mine
I want to read you poetry by candlelight
While feeding you sliced apples
And only if you're ready
I want to make you reach ecstasy
All over again

The girl he stared at blushed, the applause was as heavy as two sumo wrestlers. Mood walked off the stage to a round of applause. As the evening came to a close, everyone hung outside and talked. Hawk approached Mood saying "You never cease to amaze me, you probably got that poor girl sitting on the Metro with wet panties." They both laughed.

"I must say this is one of the best evenings this place has seen in a while." Mood said leaning against the building.

"Well you know, now that spring is here, this place will be packed with good food, fine women, and good hip-hop again well into the fall." Hawk said.

Then Mood asked. "Do you need a ride home?"

"No thanks, Dove got me."

As Mood said his goodbyes and turned to leave, a black Jetta parked across the street beeped the horn at him. He stopped to look, it was Sabrina Blake with a friend. Mood walked across the street and bent down on the driver's side.

"Hello ladies." Mood said with a deep voice.

"Hi Mood, this is my friend Melanie Street."

Melanie had a bright smile on her face and long braids on her head that she wrapped into a ponytail. "Hi." She waved.

"How was the game?" Mood asked.

"It was fun. That guy, George, was in my face the whole night. He has the worse breath. As soon as I got home I paged Melanie and we came straight here. I guess we missed the show?"

"Yeah, it was a pretty good night."

"Well, Mel and I are going to a rooftop party in Georgetown, what are you about to do?"

"I'm going home, I have to be at work at 7:00." Mood said.

"That reminds me Mr. Concierge," Sabrina smiled. "We need to be at the Georgetown Library tomorrow at 10. I'm helping Melanie study for the bar. Could you call me at 8:00?" She asked while writing her phone number on a napkin and handing it to him.

Mood grabbed the number and asked. "You're not cranky when you wake up are you?"

"You'll just have to find out." She started the car.

"I'll find out for sure. Melanie, it was a pleasure to meet you. Ladies, have a good time at the party tonight."

"Thanks." Sabrina said and they drove away.

The next day at 7:45 Mood was dressed in a gray suit with a colorful tie. "Finally Friday." He thought. Just then George walked in dressed in a brown double-breasted suit.

"Hey George, how was the game?"

"It was okay. Even though the Bullets lost, they still managed to score more than I did."

"What do you mean?" Mood asked.

"Well, Mr. Blake's daughter, Sabrina was there and I was trying to kick it with her but she wasn't interested." George said.

"Maybe if you tried a breath mint," Mood thought. "So George, what are your plans this weekend?" Mood asked. "Well," George said. "The Royal Property Management annual dinner is tonight."

"Oh yeah, I forgot that was tonight."

"Well you weren't invited, you have to be a member of the staff to attend." George said nastily and continued. "Tomorrow there's supposed to be a picnic for Royal employees and their families, I'll have another shot at Sabrina Blake."

As George got on the elevator, Mood looked at his watch. It was 8:00. Mood took the napkin out of his pocket and called Sabrina's number.

"Hello?" Sabrina said with a slight moan in her voice.

"Do you always sound so sexy at 8:00?" Mood asked.

"You should see me," She yawned and stretched. "Thanks for waking me up."

"My pleasure," Mood said, then he asked. "What's your weekend looking like?"

"I'm helping Mel study for the bar, so the majority of today will be spent at the law library. Then I'm going to the company dinner tonight. Are you going?" She asked Mood.

"No, you would have to be a member of the company to attend and I'm not a member."

"Well you can come with me. I'm gonna need somebody to chill with while I'm there. I asked Melanie and she can't make it."

"Look, I'll think about it and let you know."

"Alright, goodbye." She said.

"Goodbye." He hung up the phone and Mr. Blake arrived. Mood reached in the back and brought out five dry cleaned shirts on hangers.

"Good morning Theodore." Mr. Blake reached for the shirts. "How are you?"

"Excellent thank you, are you ready for the big dinner?" Mood asked.

"Yes I'm ready, it's going to be a very big night. All the members of the Royal Property Management family will be there. There will also be a picnic tomorrow in the Rock Creek Park."

"That's great sir, here are your messages."

Mood gave the messages to Mr. Blake and he went into the elevator.

At 11:00, Dove arrived with the mail. "You're here early today Dove." Mood checked his watch.

"Yeah I know, the mail volume's not that heavy today. Who was that honey that you were talking to in the car last night?"

"That was Mr. Blake's daughter, I just met her yesterday. She invited me to go with her to that big dinner tonight. Do you think that I should go?" Mood asked Dove.

"I don't see any reason why you shouldn't."

"The dinner's for the company and it's real exclusive, I don't want to feel uncomfortable or make her dad feel uncomfortable."

"That's bullshit! You're Mood, nobody's uncomfortable around you, go out there and be yourself and have a good time. There's nothing else going on this weekend."

"That's true," Mood said. "Dove could you do me a favor?"

At noon, Dove parked his mail truck into the driveway of Georgetown University's Law School. He walked around the campus until he found the law library. He looked around until he found Sabrina and her friend Melanie sitting at a table with a stacks of books. Sabrina was dressed in a pair of baggy cotton gray sweat pants, a pair of classic Reeboks and a red Delta Sigma Theta tee shirt. He approached her.

"Excuse me, Are you Sabrina Blake?"

"Yes I am." She said.

Dove reached into his satchel and pulled out a red rose with a note attached.

"My name's Dove and this is from Mood, he asked me to give you this."

Dove handed the items to her and left. Sabrina opened up the note, which read "I'd love to go." signed "Mood". She stared at Melanie and said. "Looks like I have a date."

"Are you sure your father wants him there?" Melanie asked.

"It's not about my daddy," Sabrina said. "Let me see how you did on that mock test I put together for you."

That night at the Grand Ballroom of the Hyatt. The Royal Property Management dinner was in full swing. In the D.C. area, Royal owned twenty properties and each property had at least seven employees. The ballroom's full of activity, Sherman Blake and his wife Jennifer Blake walked in holding hands and went to the table where many of Mr. Blake's employees sat. Mr. Blake was dressed in a black suit with a black shirt and a white tie. Mrs. Blake was dressed in a long beautiful black sequenced gown.

"Mr. and Mrs. Blake." George said wearing the same double breasted suit from earlier. "How are you? Mrs. Blake, you look beautiful." He leaned over to kiss Mrs. Blake on the cheek.

"Thank you." Mrs. Blake said as Mr. Blake pulled out her chair then he sat down, Pablo and his wife Josephine were there too.

"This place looks beautiful." Mr. Blake said looking around.

"I thought Sabrina was coming." George said as he sat down.

"Oh she'll be along soon, she had just returned from the library when we were leaving." Mrs. Blake said.

"That's good." George replied.

"George is really going places in the company, At twenty seven he has already set the tone for the future of Royal." Mr. Blake praised George.

Pablo rolled his eyes and Josephine laughed.

"I also think he would be perfect for our Sabrina."

"Thank you sir." George beamed.

Mr. Blake then turned to his wife and asked. "Honey, would you like to dance?"

"I'd love to." She said as they got up and headed towards the dance floor.

As they danced to the music, Mrs. Blake looked into her husband's eyes and smiled. "Honey, George seems like a nice guy but I don't think Sabrina would appreciate you trying to fix her up."

"Dear, George is the right man for her."

"Really, maybe she doesn't know that." She said looking towards the entrance.

Mr. Blake turned around and watched his daughter walk in dressed in a red mini dress, by her side dressed in a black suit with a white shirt and a black tie was Mood.

Mr. Blake turned around and saw them arrive. "What is she doing here with him? Why did she bring him here?"

"Who is he?" Jennifer asked.

"That's the concierge, Theodore Moody, he's the guy who answers the phone." "He's cute." Jennifer said. Mood and Sabrina walked over to the bar to get a drink. Mr. and Mrs. Blake walked back to the table. Soon Mood and Sabrina walked to the table, Mood pulled out Sabrina's chair and sat down next to her.

"Good evening everyone." Mood said looking around the table. "You must be Mrs. Blake, It's a pleasure to finally meet you." Mood shook her hand. "The pleasure's all mine and call me Jennifer, now I can put a face with your voice." Mrs. Blake smiled.

"I didn't know you knew my daughter." Mr. Blake faked a smile.

"Well I met her yesterday." Mood began.

"But I've seen him perform at The Abstract Griot."

"Oh, What do you do?" She asked.

"Well I write and perform poetry." Mood smiled.

"What do they call you the Mood man or something?" George said irritably.

"How did you get that name?" asked Mr. Blake.

"Well, when I was stationed in Saudi Arabia for Operation Desert Storm I wrote a lot of love poems for my friends to send to their girlfriends or wives. They gave me the nickname Mood and it stuck."

"Really?" Mr. Blake perked up. "What branch of service were you in?" He asked.

"I was in the Marines."

"Why did you get out?" George asked coldly.

Mood noticed his attitude. "I felt trapped and I didn't care for it too much. I don't regret going in but I found myself and the 'me' I found didn't want to be a Marine."

Pablo whispered something in Spanish into Josephine's ear. His wife laughed and looked at George, who looked upset.

Mr. Blake's face lit up. "I'm a former Marine too, Where were you stationed?" He asked.

"At Camp Lejeune, NC. What about you?"

"I spent time at Lejeune, but most of my time was spent in Quantico, VA.

How long were you in for?" Mood asked.

"I did ten years but had to get out on a medical discharge."

"Don't get Dad talking about his Marine Corps days, he'll be yapping all night." Sabrina said.

"Yeah, I've heard these stories a million times." Mrs. Blake said.

"Hush you two, we have a fellow devil dog among us." Mr. Blake smiled.

31

The waiter served roast duck with crisp paper thin slices of sweet pickled turnips, baked white potatoes, and corn on the cob. After dinner Pablo and Josephine danced, Sabrina and Mrs. Blake went to the ladies room and Mr. Blake went to the lobby to smoke a cigar with some of the other property managers. George sat alone at the table when Mood returned from the men's room and sat at the table. When George rolled his eyes Mood asked. "What's wrong George? You seem upset, Aren't you having a good time?"

"I would if you would have stayed in your place Theodore."

"What do you mean by that?" Mood asked.

"Look around you, everyone in this ballroom makes more than that pitiful salary you bring home. What is it? $19,500 a year?" He chuckled.

Mood was taken aback, someone whom he thought was his friend actually looked down on Mood as if he were beneath him.

"Oh let me get this straight, we're cool when I'm in my element but when I'm in your world, I'm considered a threat. Why are you so jealous? Is it because I pulled the girl and I don't have the Lexus in my driveway or the $45,000 salary like you? You need to be real." Mood said.

"Whatever, Hop back in your little truck and go back to your world with your little hip-hop crews."

With that said George got up and went to the bar. Sabrina and Mrs. Blake returned to the table and looked at the once crowded ballroom as it slowly emptied. Sabrina sat next to Mood and Mrs. Blake checked her watch.

"It's getting really late, I wonder where your father is?" She looked around.

"He went into the lobby with Mr. Bancroft and Mr. McCutchen." Mood answered.

"Thank you Theodore." She walked towards the lobby.

"Your moms is real cool." Mood said looking into Sabrina's eyes.

"She likes you too, she told me in the ladies' room that

you were a perfect gentleman."

"I see where you get your beauty from." Mood smiled.

Sabrina smiled. "You think I'm beautiful?"

Mood held her hand. "From the moment I saw you."

They remained silent for a few minutes, the silence was broken when Mrs. Blake returned. "Honey, Sherman and I are about to leave. Would you like to ride with us or are you O.K.?"

"I'm O.K. Mommy." She said not taking her eyes off of Mood.

"Goodnight, Theodore."

Mood broke eye contact stood up and took Mrs. Blake's hand. "Goodnight Mrs. Blake, take care of yourself."

The band played the final song of the evening, a jazzy rendition of Janet Jackson's *Anytime*. "We haven't danced all evening." Mood said.

"I know, I figured you were afraid I'd show you up on the dance floor." Sabrina joked.

"No, I'd rather you look me in my eyes while we danced and not at my feet trying to copy my moves." Mood joked back.

"What are we waiting for?" He stood up and took her hand. They held each other close as they danced and looked into each other's eyes. They held each other tighter as they got into a rhythmic slow grind. Mood closed his eyes as he got a scent of her perfume. George watched from the bar as they danced, he finished his drink and left in anger. Mood and Sabrina didn't even notice, they were in their own world.

At noon on Saturday, Mood's pager woke him out of a deep sleep. He looked at the number, reached for the phone and dialed.

"Did someone page Theodore?" He asked groggily.

"Still dreaming about last night sleepyhead?"

The sound of Sabrina's voice brought Mood to full attention. "Just dreaming about you." He said.

"Wow, you're even smooth with morning breath." She

laughed at her own joke.

"Where are you?" Mood asked when he heard all of the noise in the background.

"I'm here at my dad's company picnic. "She said.

"I bet every male there is wearing beige khaki pants." Mood said turning on the television with the remote control.

"Don't fake like you don't own a pair." She said. "Look, I was reading the *D.C. City Reader* last night. The Key in Georgetown is playing two of Dorothy Dandridge's movies *Carmen Jones* and Porgy and Bess at 3:00. Do you want to go see them?"

"I'd love to, do you need me to pick you up?"

"Yeah, I rode down here with my parents."

"No problem, I'll meet you on Connecticut Avenue at the Rock Creek Park entrance at 2:30." Mood said.

"I'll be there, goodbye."

Mood hung up the phone and looked at his watch. "I have a few hours." He thought as he began to straighten up his studio apartment. After he showered and ate, he found a pair of baggy black jeans, a blue denim shirt and his pair of beige Timberlands. He sat back down in front of the television and flipped channels. He stopped when he found a Kung Fu movie on Channel 50. When it ended at 2:00, he hopped into his Isuzu Trooper and headed for Rock Creek Park. When he arrived Sabrina was there waiting drinking a can of Sprite. She wore a pair of black stretch pants, a gray Tommy Hilfiger tee shirt, a pair of white classic Reeboks and a black denim Levi's jacket.

When Mood pulled up she started walking towards the truck, All Mood could think was "DAMMMMN!" as she climbed into the truck.

"Hey Mood." She pulled off her jacket and put on her seatbelt. "You thirsty?"

"No, What's up with you?"

"Nothing, Thanks for coming to get me. Melanie's all up in her man's face this weekend so she doesn't want to do anything."

"It's cool, I love Dorothy Dandridge but I've only seen Carmen Jones." Mood. said.

The radio played *Top Billin'* by Audio Two. "Oh that's my joint!" Mood said excitedly as he turned up the radio. "This is the song that made me a hip-hop head." He bobbed his head and rhymed along with the song.

"Well the song that made me a hip-hop head was LL Cool J's *I Need Love*." Sabrina. said.

"I used to rock a Kangol like that back in the day." Mood laughed.

Sabrina laughed. They were at the Key in no time. Mood and Sabrina sat in the back of the crowded theater and shared a big tub of popcorn. The first movie they played was *Carmen Jones*.

Near the end of the movie Sabrina grabbed Mood's hand. "This is the part where he kills her." Mood puts his arm around her to comfort her. As Harry Belafonte sang the final song of the movie, tears came streaming down Sabrina's cheeks.

"It's so sad, He never knew how much she really loved him."

"I know." Mood said wiped her tears. He reached over to kiss her tenderly on the lips. She responded by pulling him closer and sticking her tongue in his mouth. They shared a long lingering kiss and missed the opening credits to *Porgy and Bess*.

After the movie, they enjoyed a beautiful spring evening by driving to Haines Point. Mood reached into the back of the truck and grabbed a blanket. They walked until they found a well lit area where they sat and looked up into the sky. Under the moonlight Mood read poetry by his favorite poet, Langston Hughes. Soon after they got up and began to walk around the park beside the river.

"Mood?" Sabrina said breaking the silence.

"Yes sweetheart" Mood said holding her from behind.

"Do you think this is going too fast? I mean we've only

been out last night and today and I just need to know if this is just a weekend thing, I mean what's going on here?"

"Well," Mood began. "What are you looking for in a relationship?"

She was silent for a minute, then answered. "I'm looking for romance, fun, independence, freedom to love honestly, respect and a lot of communication."

"Well, honestly, I don't think one can put a time line on feelings."

"It's just that I've never met anyone like you before." Sabrina said. "I mean a lot of guys fake shit like this just to get a woman into bed, but you've been a gentleman. I can look in your eyes and see your sincerity."

"How do you feel?" Mood asked.

"I feel really good being with you, but I begin work for Duffy Law in Chicago in May, I should be concentrating on my career. But I do like you a lot." She said still facing the water.

"I feel your career is very important and I don't want to interfere with that. Let's take this at a pace you're comfortable with until May. Let's take this one day at a time O.K.?"

"O.K." Sabrina said. Mood looked at his watch and said. "It's getting close to 11:00, Is there anything else you feel like doing tonight?"

"No, I'd better be getting home."

Mood drove Sabrina back to her parent's house in Fort Washington, a suburb of D.C. When they pulled into the driveway Mood asked. "What are you doing tomorrow?"

"Well I have to help Melanie study. Why?"

"Tomorrow is poetry night at The Abstract Griot, Why don't you come by and I'll buy you dinner. You can meet some of my friends."

"I'd love to." She said as she reached over and gave Mood a kiss and got out of the truck. He waited for her to go inside before he pulled out of the driveway and drove home.

On Sunday night, The Abstract Griot was packed as usual. Mood had signed in to do some spoken word and waited at a booth for Sabrina to arrive.

"Hey Mood," Dove slid into the booth. "How was your date with Sabrina?"

"It went well, she's supposed to be coming through tonight."

"Word! That's good."

"Where's your partner in rhyme Hawk at?" Mood asked.

"He went to check out Rare Essence at the Bomb Shelter. I'll be back, I've got to take a piss." Dove got up to leave.

Paradise and Dana came in. Mood saw them and called them over. They walked over to the table and sat down. "Hey Mood, What's up?" Dana asked.

"Yeah, we haven't seen you all weekend. You missed AntiGravity's performance here last night."

"Well I met a girl last week at work and I've been spending some time with her, I'm meeting her here tonight. I think she may be the one."

Dana and Paradise looked at each other, they couldn't hold back their laughter. "The one?" Dana said. "Mood I hate to say this but I don't think you're the one woman type."

"What does that mean?" Mood said offended by the comment.

"Don't be mad Mood," Paradise said. "You're just not the monogamous type. Remember last year when you were dating the two cousins and one didn't know you were dating the other?"

"Yeah, you invited one here for poetry night and the other one showed up to surprise you." Dana said.

"You must have read every poem you had that night, you did anything to stay on that stage so you wouldn't have to confront either one of them. When they discovered the truth, they slashed two of your tires." Paradise continued.

"Yeah but this is different." Mood said. "There was a connection there that I can't explain, it was cosmic."

"Mood I love you like a brother, but I wouldn't date

37

your ass." Dana said.

"Yeah, because that damn charm of yours is dangerous." Paradise laughed. "And we're not even gonna bring up the fucking contest with your old Marine Corps friends."

"Oh yeah, I totally forgot about that." Dana said.

"O.K. ladies, you made your point but I can change. You'll see."

"Yeah, we'll see." Dana said as they got up and went to the bar where Kenny was.

Mood sighed as he thought about his past relationships. Was he really that much of a dog? Mood looked up and saw Sabrina walk in wearing a pair of jeans, a pair of sneakers and a white shirt. She looked around until she made eye contact with Mood, she walked over to the table and gave Mood a kiss on the cheek. Dana and Paradise watched from the bar and filled Kenny in on the new Mood. Kenny laughed at the thought of putting the words "Mood" and "monogamy" together. When Jacob came to take their orders, Mood ordered the fried chicken and candy yams. Sabrina ordered the chicken salad. Later that evening, Mood and Sabrina sat at the table and talked and laughed as Paradise, Dana, Kenny and Dove watched from the bar. They noticed a different Mood.

"Maybe it can work, he seems different around her. More attentive, more affectionate." Dana said.

Paradise agreed. "Maybe you can teach an old dog new tricks."

Toni called Mood on stage to read, when he got to the microphone he said. "Good evening. I want to dedicate this poem to all the beautiful Nubian Queens.

Whoever invented the upright bass
Must've been inspired by you,
   Black Woman.

He must've held your beautiful curves one night.
He felt the magic when he caressed that beautiful

Mahogany Brown Skin

He must've made love to you Black Woman
When he fingered your strings
He made you moan beautiful music
    Black Woman

The bass was Mingus' mistress too
When he played you he traveled to constellations
Before returning home to his wife of European descent.

Whoever invented the upright bass
Must have been inspired by you
    Black Woman

He must've placed his bow on your chords
To make you moan louder, different, more rhythmic.
The faster you're stroked
The louder the sound
Until the improvisational climax

Silence until the crowd applauds
He wipes the sweat with a towel,
Lights a cigarette,
And softly whispers
Was it good for you?

After Mood completed his poem, the crowd rose and
clapped. He returned to the booth and asked. "How did you
like my poem?"

"I thought it was pretty fly." She said.

"I think you're pretty fly." He said as he reached over
to kiss her.

Dana, Paradise, Kenny, and Dove looked in Mood's
direction. "I told you I think he really likes this girl." Dove
said.

At the table, Mood held her hand and told her. "I want

to be monogamous with you. I can't get you off my mind, I'm willing to do whatever I have to including not standing in the way of your career. Are you ready?"

"I think I am, but I leave for Chicago soon."

"Well let's just enjoy every day together, Are you willing to give me that commitment?"

Sabrina nodded yes. "Good see those people sitting over there at the bar?" He pointed to his friends. "I want you to meet them."

They left the table and went to the bar.

"Kenny, Dana, Dove, Paradise. I would like you to meet Sabrina."

DANA CONNERS

The alarm buzzed loud and sharp as Dana rose from her sleep. Squinting her eyes and trying to focus on the time she read the clock 7:00. After she turned on the radio to WSOL, she forced herself out the bed and stumbled to the bathroom to take a shower. After the shower she put on the white shirt and skirt that she ironed. She returned to the bathroom to tied her long raven black hair into a bun and applied a small amount of lipstick. Dana debated whether she should wear the flats or the pumps. After deciding on the flats, she inspected herself in the mirror. Dana, who stood five feet eight inches tall with honey brown skin and deep brown eyes felt she had made the right choice. "Professional enough." She thought. Just then the phone rang, she knew who it was before she looked at the caller ID.

"Good morning Mommy."

"Hi baby, I'm not gonna hold you. I just called to say good luck at the new school."

"Thanks Mommy."

"Be careful, I've been hearing about those D.C. schools on the news. How they're run down and I even heard about that principal who got into a fight with that reporter."

"How did you hear about that? You live in South Carolina."

"Girl I got CNN, make sure you watch your back."

"I will Mommy, you better get off this phone. You know how much long distance calls cost this time of day." Dana checked her watch. "I know you hang out with those rappers, Don't teach those kids Ebonics like that teacher in Oakland."

"I love you Mommy goodbye." Dana laughed.

"Bye Baby."

She hung up the phone, grabbed her jacket and was on

her way out the door. She thought about breakfast but quickly declined, she was too nervous to eat. Today was her first day at a new school. She'll be teaching her own sixth grade class.

It was a pleasant, sunny spring morning as Dana walked a block from her Sutton Walk apartment complex to the New Carrolton Metro. She couldn't help but be excited. After three years as a substitute teacher in a suburban Maryland school, she received the offer to teach her own class at Andrew Jackson Elementary School. Dana was thrilled, as much as she hated to leave her old school she knew she had excelled as far as possible there. This transfer means her career was taking off. She waited for the orange line train to arrive and got on board. After she got off the Metro at Minnesota Ave., the school was across the street from the Metro. She walked toward the school, As she passed the schoolyard, she peered inside the fenced in yard. The school walls were defaced with graffiti, the ground was covered with shards of glass and empty crack vials were everywhere. The boys were playing basketball on a hoop with no net and the girls were playing jump rope. Other children just hung around waiting for the school bell to ring. A police officer was walking the schoolyard grounds keeping those who did not belong there away.

Dana walked into the front entrance of the school and went to the attendance office. She heard a gruff voice behind her. "You must be Ms. Conners, we've been expecting you."

She turned to greet a balding, short white man with a potbelly.

"It's a pleasure to meet you, we spoke on the phone. I'm Edward Wright, the principal."

"Nice to meet you." Dana tried to conceal her amusement. After their phone conversation, she expected him to be completely different.

"Please come with me to my office and I'll brief you

on your class and class assignments."

As they entered the office Mr. Wright poured a cup of coffee for himself and pulled a doughnut out of a box of Dunkin' Donuts near the coffeepot.

"You're welcome to help yourself." He offered.

"No thank you, I had a big breakfast." Dana lied.

Mr. Wright sat down at his desk, grabbed a file and said. "You'll be taking over class 216, that was Mr. Stevens' class. They're in the process of learning long division. Their last history assignment was on Custer's Last Stand and they have a book report due today on the book of their choice."

He handed her the curriculum, a classroom key and the attendance list as he rose from his chair and said. "Welcome to Andrew Jackson Elementary."

Dana rose, shook his hand and said. "Thank you."

As she turned to leave Mr. Wright said. "And good luck."

Dana entered room 216 and surveyed the classroom. It had six rows of desks and five desks across, her seat was directly in front. The window was to her right and behind the back row was a closet full of hooks for students to hang their coats. There was an American flag above the chalkboard next to a clock that told her it was 8:35. According to Mr. Wright the class was supposed to begin in five minutes. "I've got five minutes to get myself together." She thought nervously. At 8:40. fourteen boys and sixteen girls came into the room. The boys discussed last night's Washington Bullets game, while the girls argued over which member of Dru Hill they liked the most. They hung up their jackets and sat at their desks and looked at Dana.

"Good morning class, my name is Ms. Conners." She turned and wrote her name on the blackboard. "I'll be your teacher for the remainder of the year." So far everything was going nicely. "I'll be taking attendance now."

She ran through the list of names. "Jeanette?" "Here." "Jose?" "Here."

She noticed that all of the names were in alphabetical order. When Dana had finished, she asked for the book reports that were due. After receiving and counting them she realized that she only had twenty nine reports in front of her.

"Who didn't turn in a book report?" She asked.

A skinny brown skinned boy named Oliver raised his hand and said. "It was me, I left it at home but I'll have it tomorrow Ms. Conners."

"If it's not in by tomorrow you will receive an 'F' Oliver." Dana said.

"Yes ma'am!" Oliver said. He knew another "F" would mean another whipping. He made sure that he wouldn't forget.

At 9:00 Dana asked the students to rise and say the *Pledge of Allegiance*. Afterwards a young black boy dressed in blue jeans, a black shirt and a pair of run down Nikes raised his hand.

"Yes Hakeem?" Dana asked.

"Why do we pledge allegiance to that flag and not the flag of our motherland of Africa?"

She couldn't believe that such a deep question could come from an eleven year old boy. She answered. "Many of our forefathers fought to make equality a reality for our people. Many people from our motherland were brought here and enslaved. Once they became free, they believed in the basic principles that this flag represented and still represents. Many fought and died for this country. When we pledge allegiance, we honor them as well. Do you understand?"

"Yes, that makes sense." He said.

Dana taught the class long division and gave them a spelling quiz, soon the class was dismissed for lunch. As they left, Dana's attention was drawn to an eleven year old brown skinned girl with curly hair named Lisa Morgan. Lisa had not participated in class all morning and just stared at the floor. Jeanette, the girl who sat directly in front of Dana spoke.

"Hakeem asks every teacher that same question, he does that to see what kind of answer he'll get. Your answer was the first he liked."

Dana smiled as Jeanette leave the room. Then she looked for Lisa but she already left the room. Dana spent her lunch break in the teacher's cafeteria, she bought a bottle of spring water, a cheeseburger and some fries. She chose a table in the back and sat with her back towards the window. The gentle breeze from the window felt good as she relaxed, kicked her shoes off under the table and started to eat her lunch.

"Welcome to Andrew Jackson." A female voice with an accent greeted her.

Dana looked up from her lunch and saw an older woman who wore a business suit and had her hair twisted in a tight bun, she carried a salad on a tray.

"My name is Rosita Jenkins, I teach the third grade class in room 112. What's your name?" She asked.

"I'm Dana Conners, I've taken over Mr. Steven's sixth grade class." She said.

"I'm glad they finally found someone to teach that class, there have been substitute teachers in and out of that room for over a month." Rosita said.

"I just hope I do a good job." Dana liked Rosita and knew that they would become good friends. "Well, all the students have warmed up to me except Lisa Morgan, she's hardly spoken two words and didn't participate in class all morning."

Rosita looked at the big clock on the wall and said. "That's odd when she was in my class she wasn't very shy, trust me she'll come around. The bell is about to ring and I have to beat the kids back to class or they'll never let me live it down. I'll see you soon."

Rosita was gone before Dana could utter another word. Dana looked up at the clock and couldn't believe what time it was. She hurried, finished her spring water, and rushed back to her classroom. The kids were settled down and ready to begin their history lesson by the time Dana returned to class.

"Everyone turn your history books to page 158."

She was almost through the details of Custer's Last Stand when Hakeem raised his hand.

"Yes Hakeem?" Dana asked.

"Why did they send General Custer's Army to kill the Indians? They weren't harming anyone, this is their land ain't it?"

Dana patiently answered. "The U.S. Government misunderstood the Native Americans and people fear what they don't understand. This spawns hate and prejudice, America has done this time and time again, this is why prejudice still exist today."

"That makes a lot of sense." Hakeem said.

That night at The Abstract Griot Dana walked in wearing blue jeans and a blue denim shirt. When she saw Flame and Paradise in one of the booths, she walked over and gave her girls a hug, the three had met at the club and had established a tight bond of sisterhood. Dana sat down and looked around.

"This place usually is not crowded on a Monday night. What's going on?"

"That girl is celebrating her twenty first birthday," Paradise pointed to her. "I think she brought all of Howard U. with her."

"Damn!" Flame said. "If I could do twenty one again, I would have graduated college instead of bullshittin'."

"You're not bullshitting," Dana reassured her friend. "Give it time, school's not going anywhere."

"That's true." Paradise said twisting her hair.

"That's easy for y'all to say, y'all got degrees."

"So Dana, how was your first day at Andrew Jackson Elementary?" Paradise changed the subject.

"Well," Dana said. "After I finally got over my butterflies it turned out to be very nice, these kids are so smart it's scary."

"Well make sure you nourish their young minds because everything you say and do effects their future." Flame said.

"Gee thanks just add to the pressure." Dana joked.

Kenny came over to greet the girls, he looked directly into Dana's eyes and said. "I heard about the new job, congratulations!"

"Thank you." Dana said.

"Have you decided on dinner yet?"

"Not yet, I haven't even looked at the menu." She smiled.

"Well it's on me tonight, sort of like a congratulations thing." Kenny smiled back.

"Thank you, Kenny."

Flame and Paradise said in unison. "Hi Kenny."

Kenny broke out of his trance. "Hello ladies, always a pleasure." He left and headed for the kitchen.

"What's up with 'I haven't looked over the menu'? Flame said. You know that whole menu like the back of your hand."

"Yeah girl," Paradise chimed in. "Plus you get a free meal, I didn't even get that when I started my new job. When are the two of you going to go out?"

"You know we're just friends, I've been coming here since his Dad owned the place. I was a junior at Howard and he was waiting and bussing tables." She smiled. "But if he were to ever ask I wouldn't say no."

"I hope not." Flame said.

Laughter surrounded the table. Flame looked up and saw Dove walk in. "There's Dove Yo! I'll be right back."

Flame walked up to Dove and said. "What's up, Dove? Why are you still in your uniform?"

"I just got off work, Mondays are usually heavy, I'm not even staying I called Kenny and ordered three plates to go. My wife was too tired to cook, Kenny said it would be ready by the time I got here."

"Does that guy from Power Records still live on your

47

route?" Flame asked.

"Yeah."

"How well do you know him?"

"It's tough to judge, we talk about music all the time. I've invited him here but he never comes, I guess he's too busy."

Flame handed him a tape. "This is our demo."

"Word! Can I listen to it?" Dove asked.

"Yeah that's cool." Kenny came out with Dove's orders.

"Hey Dove, how was your day?"

"Hectic, what's the damage?"

"That's twenty dollars," Kenny took the money and said. "Take care of yourself Dove." He disappeared back into the kitchen.

Dove watched the girl blow out the candles on her birthday cake and said. "Man if I could do twenty one again."

"I feel you Dove." She hugged him goodbye and watched him leave. When Flame got back to the table Dana and Paradise were ready to order. "I'll just have the cheese fries." Flame said. Paradise ordered the baked beans and fried chicken. Dana had the baked ham and candy yams. They laughed and enjoyed the evening.

For the rest of the week Dana spent time trying to get to acquainted with the students. She got along well with everyone except Lisa, who was still withdrawn. On Thursday Dana asked the class. "What do you want to be when you grow up?" Dana heard shouts of fireman, cop, and even Army soldier.

"Doesn't anyone want to be a doctor or lawyer or something that requires a college education?"

"Mr. Stevens told us to forget college." Jose' said.

Dana was shocked. "What! When did he tell you this?"

"All the time." Analisa said.

"I can't believe this, you children can be and do anything you want. Look at me, I've achieved something. I'm a teacher and I have one of the most rewarding jobs there is educating future leaders. Every one of you has something wonderful and unique to offer the world. How many of you know who Malcolm X is?"

Hands went in the air.

"Denzel Washington." One kid screamed out and the class laughed.

"Malcolm X was a great civil rights leader, when he was about your age he wanted to be a lawyer. His teacher discouraged him and told him that there were no nigger lawyers. That teacher was wrong just like Mr. Stevens is wrong. Malcolm X went on to become a great man. That's why he's in your history books today. Even Nelson Mandela was jailed for twenty three years and he became the President of South Africa."

"Yeah and Marion Barry smoked crack and still became mayor." Jose said. The class began to laugh.

"What else did Mr. Stevens ask you to keep secret?" Dana noticed that Lisa suddenly looked away towards the window while trying to hold back the tears that were streaming down her cheeks. The hurt that Dana saw on her young face nearly broke Dana's heart. "Lisa, follow me into the hall please. Class, I'll be right back, Jeanette you're in charge until I get back."

In the hall Dana handed Lisa a napkin and asked her. "What's wrong Lisa? All week long you've been withdrawn. Is there something you want to tell me?"

Lisa's eyes dropped to the floor and she shook her head no.

"I want to be your friend, you can trust me." Lisa backed against the wall in fear. "No don't say that to me. That's what Mr. Stevens said before he…"

Dana was confused. "What? What did he do to you?" Dana became impatient.

"He touched me." She finally said and she began crying harder. "He's gonna get my little sister, he told me if I ever told he's gonna get my little sister."

49

Dana was stunned and speechless, She crouched down to make eye contact with Lisa. "I'm scared Ms. Conners."

"How long has this been going on?" Dana asked fighting her own tears.

"He did it twice and then he was gone."

"I won't let him hurt you or your sister. Go get your books and your coat and go home, you need to go home and tell your mother. Don't be scared, you didn't do anything wrong. Mr. Stevens is to blame for this not you."

"I can't tell her, I don't know what to say. What if she doesn't believe me?" Then she looked up at Dana. "Can you tell them please?" Lisa begged her.

"Alright." After Lisa left, Dana gained her composure and walked back into the classroom. She looked at her watch, it was time to dismiss the class for the day.

"Children listen up! There will be no homework tonight, I will see you tomorrow."

After everyone left Dana went to the ladies room to regain her composure. She experienced so many emotions at once and wanted to be calm when she spoke to Mr. Wright. She walked to his office and found him sitting at his desk going over the cafeteria's budget. She knocked on the door.

Mr. Wright looked up and smiled. "Ms. Conners have a seat, How's your first week here with us?"

She sat down across the desk from him. "It's been a learning experience," She said. "What happened to Mr. Stevens?"

"Mr. Stevens is working for Wayne High School in Bethesda. He was offered more money and from what I understand he loves it, he's even coaching the girl's basketball team." Mr. Wright said proudly.

Dana braced herself and said. "Mr. Wright, Mr. Stevens touched Lisa Morgan in an improper manner and it's affecting her school performance. When I asked her what was wrong, she told me about it today."

Mr. Wright gasped in shock. "I'm surprised to hear

this. Are you sure she's not lying?"

"I can tell by the way she's acting and I believe her."

"Why hasn't she mentioned this before?"

"She was scared because he threatened her little sister." Dana said.

"These are very serious accusations to make but I assure you if they are true Mr. Stevens will pay for his actions against that poor child. Thank you Ms. Conners, I will notify the principal of Wayne High School." Mr. Wright said.

"Thank you for your time Mr. Wright, if I can be of any further assistance please let me know." She rose to leave.

Dana returned to her classroom to prepare Friday's lessons. There was a knock on the door, Rosita walked in and sat on Jeanette's desk.

"I heard how you took up for Lisa, but there's something you should know. About a month before Mr. Stevens left, I overheard him and Mr. Wright in Mr. Wright's office. They didn't know I was standing outside his door. I heard Mr. Stevens bragging about what he'd done with a student but I didn't know which student. It made me sick to my stomach to hear Mr. Wright laugh along with him."

"What!" Dana exclaimed. "I can't believe this! What's gonna happen now?"

"The most you can do is talk to her parents and persuade them to take legal action. Mr. Wright is not going to do anything," Rosita rose to leave. "I have to go, my husband should be downstairs waiting for me."

As Rosita left, Dana rose to her feet, sat on the edge of her desk, sank her head into her hands and cried.

After heavy debate, Dana decided to go to The Abstract Griot where the jazz band Soul Call was fresh from its tour of Europe. They performed some contemporary jazz and thrilled the audience with tales from abroad. Mood and Sabrina sat at one of the cozy tables and held hands as they enjoyed the show. Mood saw Dana sitting alone and looking distant in a corner booth. She hadn't touched her food or paid the band any attention. Since Antigravity had a show at the 9:30 Club, Flame and Paradise weren't around. Kenny was upstairs in his office trying to contact members of Nomad, his dad's old band members.

Mood said to Sabrina. "Excuse me for a moment." And walked to Dana's table.

"Hey Dana." He said standing over the table.

"Hey Mood, you two make a cute couple." Dana said.

"Thanks, you look bothered. Are you okay?" Mood asked concerned.

"Yeah just a bad day at work."

"Do you feel like talking?"

"No I'm cool." She lied.

"Okay." Mood said he walked upstairs past all of the artwork to Kenny's office and knocked on his door.

"Come in." Kenny said still on the phone. Mood sat while Kenny tried to hurry his phone conversation. After he finished, Kenny asked Mood. "Is everything okay?"

"Yeah but you should go downstairs and talk to Dana, something's bothering her and she's not trying to talk to me about it. I figured she'd talk to you."

"Well I'll try."

"Thank you Kenny, I better get back downstairs."

Kenny followed Mood downstairs and saw Dana, she looked real irritated, he walked over to the booth and sat across from her. "Hi Dana."

"Hi Kenny." She said not looking up at him.

"I need you to come with me." He grabbed her hand and took her upstairs to his office, they sat down on the small office sofa. "I know something's bothering you, Do you want to talk?" He asked.

She looked Kenny in the eyes and explained the situation to him as she wiped the tears from her eyes. "I feel so helpless." She said.

"Well, she obviously saw something because she confided in you and no one else. I can't tell you what to do but I think your friend Rosita had the right idea. Her parents should be told what happened and urged to press charges." He grabbed a tissue from the box of Kleenex and wiped her tears.

"Thank you Kenny, I'm so glad we talked." When she reached over to hug him he closed his eyes and held her tight, this was the closest he had ever been to her and he cherished the moment.

She checked her watch. "I'd better go, I have a big day tomorrow."

"Here are the numbers to the office and my apartment. Call me if you wish to talk some more, it doesn't matter what time, I'll be there for you."

"Thanks Kenny, goodnight." He looked out of the window and watched her until she was out of sight.

On Friday at 4:00, class was dismissed for the weekend. Dana, dressed in a red pantsuit, white blouse and a red scarf that she tied around her neck received a visit from Lisa's parents. Dana greeted Mr. Morgan, he was a tall black man, who was completely bald and had a full beard. "I'm Bill Morgan." He said. His breath told Dana he was drunk. "And this is my wife Sally."

She looked like Lisa except that she wore her hair in braids and wore eyeglasses. Dana asked them to sit down and explained the reason for their visit. "I'm sure you're wondering why I asked you both here," She said. "I want to talk to you about Lisa's old teacher Mr. Stevens."

As Dana told them the situation, she witnessed a series of emotions from surprise to pain and then to sorrow. Sally couldn't stop crying and Bill kept repeating. "I don't understand how this can happen in school, a place of learning!"

Dana felt their pain. "If you want to press charges against Mr. Stevens I'll be there and I'll help all I can."

Sally spoke for the first time as she wiped her tears. "Look Ms. Conners, I appreciate what you are trying to do, but we'll handle this ourselves." As she rose to leave Dana felt helpless but managed to say. "I hope everything works out." Mr. Morgan slowly walked out behind his wife.

Dana rode the train home in silence. When she arrived, she drew a bubble bath, undressed in her bedroom and kicked her clothes into a pile by the clothes hamper. She stepped into the tub and let the water engulf her. Tears streamed down her face as she recalled the events of the past week. She hoped she made a difference.

HAWK AND DOVE

On Saturday night at 11:00, Kenny and Jacob moved all of the tables and chairs into the closed kitchen. They cleared the floor while DJ Expression set up his Technic 1200's, cross fader and speakers on both sides of the stage. Kenny dimmed the lights to give The Abstract Griot a club like setting. By midnight, The Abstract Griot was packed with people mostly from Howard University. Everyone on the temporary dance floor was doing the wop, the Biz Mark, the boggle, the happy feet and the cabbage patch, while DJ Expression played a series of old school jams. Paradise and Hawk were dancing together while Dove, dripping with sweat from dancing, sat at the bar drinking a glass of water. When DJ Expression mixed Brand Nubian's "Slow Down" with Special Ed's "I got it made" everybody on the dance floor yelled. "Hoooo." Like a Pied Piper, the music magically carried Dove back to the floor doing the played out East coast stomp. DJ Expression mixed in some go-go,"Sardines and Pork n' Beans" and then "Booty Call." Dove danced alone when he felt a tap on his shoulder, he turned around to see a fly Latina girl dancing behind him. They began grinding rhythmically to the music. Hawk got behind him and whispered. "Keep it up and I'm telling Victoria."

"Whatever." Dove laughed.

Hawk and Dove have been best friends since their sophomore year at Duke Ellington School of the Arts. They discovered that they had a mutual love for hip-hop music and clicked during a lunchroom battle where their rhyme bout against each other ended up in a tie. Over the years they rhymed all over the D.C. area no matter what the event. They even freestyled at Dove's wedding. Their rhyme style was so off the wall that labels were scared to touch them. As a result, they were often passed up for the basic dime a dozen gangsta nihilism. It was almost 1a.m. when Antigravity walked in fresh from the studio. FOG grabbed a seat at the end of the bar and asked Kenny for some orange juice. Kenny handed him the juice.

"Hey Kenny, this club thing is a really good idea." FOG said.

"Thanks," Kenny said. "It gives these cats someplace to go and have fun without having to worry about the usual bullshit dress code and drama. When I was in college, I always got turned away because I would refuse to wear shoes, I lived in my Adidas."

"I know what you mean, there are clubs like the Ritz and D.C. Live that have rappers doing shows there and you still have to go through the no athletic gear, no jeans and boots bullshit. But why do you do it just once a month?" FOG asked.

"Have you seen these bags under my eyes? Last month, one of the cooks literally had to bang on my door upstairs so I could get Sunday brunch started."

"I feel you." Dove said.

DJ Expression threw on the instrumental from Gangstarr's Mass Appeal. FOG turned to see his friends form a huddle in the middle of the dance floor.

"Yo Kenny, I'll be right back, I think they're about to freestyle." FOG approached the small cipher and immediately joined the huddle.

FLAME:
This cipher reminds me of Buddy, Flame's the lady like Monie
The cipher 360 degrees, surround sound like Sony
I've been rhyming for a while so there's nothing you can show me
From the banks of the Nile I walk like an Egyptian
My similes cause conniptions
Giving you heart attacks like Fred G. Sanford

Rocking college tours from Howard U. to Stanford
That's in Cali. I can rhyme at The Griot but not at Blues
Alley
Bustin' Rhymes like Trevor Smith, I got gifts like Christmas
My rap class is over, You're dismissed.

HAWK:
It must be the freestyle making you shiver
Rhymes I deliver, You steady Robbin like Quivers
Broken microphones will be the clues you discover
You'll find me home on Thursday night watching New York
Undercover
I'm a Lethal Weapon like Danny Glover
Making you Dream On like Martin Tupper
And when you're awake, Reality will smack you in the face
Getting live on Saturday night like my name is Chevy Chase.

DYNAMITE:
Ease back, relax, cause you're in tune
Blowing up like balloons but I won't go pop
Because the rhymes I drop, reminds you why you love hip-
hop
And you don't stop
I miss Biggie and Tupac
Rest in Peace, I slam like the Iron Sheik
Making you feel the pain for weeks.

FOG:
Pull out my rhyme saber as I approach the Dragon's Lair
Making emcees say their prayers
Ghettos of the mind got me searching for tomorrow with
little faith
Always finishing in last place
I pray to the superior being that I'm seeing in my 3rd eye
Thinking like Mary I'm not gonna cry.

RAINDANCE:
I heard the same song on the radio
A total of 40 times a day
Wack emcees with nothing to say
Without delay I scribble rhymes
Destined to save hip-hop from decay
But the pop songs subliminally try to move my pen
This is not the end, I will fight until I win
Good vs. Evil the prize: Freedom of expression.

PARADISE:
How do I love thee
Let me count back to negative four
Because you don't respect me anymore
Where's the drama coming from
From the lies, that caused our love boat to capsize
And now I'm stranded on an Island full of broken dreams
Trying to repair my heart with bamboo and vines
Tiptoeing trying to avoid the land mines
And would I ever admit it was all worth it
And at this price, Would I ever commit
To the bullshit.

DOVE:
BIG and PAC is dead now I'm trying to stay alive like the
Bee Gees
My rhymes are funkier than feces
Lyrically, I'm like a locomotive doing the locomotion
My style is as vast as the Atlantic Ocean
You say you wanna battle you better back up off me
I got more flavor than Starbuck's Coffee
In my ear like Craig Mack, making you ease back
Like Joe Friday, I only want the facts
Save all the bullshit for your next hit
Before you battle me you better quit.

Suddenly Dove felt a vibration on his hip, he looked at the number on his pager. He didn't recognize the number but the code that belonged to his wife, Victoria, was on the end of the number. He ran upstairs to the payphone and dailed it.

"Prince George's Hospital Center." Said the voice on the other line.

"I got a page from a Mrs. Victoria Hall."

"Hold on please."

"Lawrence, Julia's sickle cell is acting up." Victoria said frantically. "I called 911 and they sent an ambulance and brought us here, they want to keep her overnight."

"Oh my God! I'm on my way." Dove said nervously.

"How are you going to get here?" Julia asked. "The car's at the house, I rode in the ambulance."

"I'll get there, Are you okay?"

"No, I'm a wreck." She said.

"I'm on my way." Dove hung up the phone and ran downstairs. There he found FOG, Hawk and Paradise sitting in a booth. Flame and Raindance were on the dance floor while Dynamite was at the bar talking to Kenny and drinking a glass of water.

"FOG, I need a big favor. I need a ride to the PG Hospital Center, my little girl had to be rushed to the hospital."

"Word! Is Julia O.K.?" Hawk asked.

"I don't know but I need a ride there." Dove said nervously.

"I'll take you." FOG said rising from the booth.

"I'm coming too." Hawk said.

At the hospital Dove, Hawk and FOG entered the children's ward and saw Victoria sitting in the waiting room. She was dressed in a pair of sweat pants, a long tee shirt and a New York Yankees baseball cap. Dove walked over to her and hugged her 5'2" frame. "Are you okay?"

"Yeah, they're going to have to keep her overnight though."

"I should've been there." Dove felt guilty.

"You should've been, I don't understand it." She cried. "You spend more time hanging out with your friends than your family, I was a complete wreck and I needed you there."

Dove couldn't say anything, he just hung his head and said. "Well I'm here now, I'm gonna ask FOG to give me a ride home so I can get the car, I'll come back."

FOG, Dove and Hawk piled back into FOG's red Amigo and drove towards Dove's house in Greenbelt, MD. Dove turned to Hawk, who sat in the back seat, and said. "Hawk, we need to have a talk."

"What's up man?" Hawk leaned forward from the back seat.

"I've been thinking man," Dove began. "I may need to take a break from this rap shit for a while and spend some time with my family. Especially with Julia's sickle cell and all, I hate to put you in this position."

"It's cool, I understand. We can take a break from rhyming for a while, you handle your business. When you come back we'll pick up right where we left off, we're boys."

FOG remained silent.

"Thanks," Dove said. "I knew you'd understand. FOG, take a left up this street here."

FOG turned. "Here it is on the right side." Dove pointed to his split level home.

"Thanks a lot FOG." Dove said as he hugged him.

"Peace Dove, I'll be praying for Julia." Dove got out and let Hawk climb into the front seat. "Thanks a lot for understanding Hawk."

"Just let me know what's up with Julia."

FOG and Hawk drove off and got on the BW Parkway towards D.C.

"So what are you going to do now?" FOG asked.

"I don't know," Hawk said. "Maybe play the D.L. until Dove is ready to rhyme again."

FOG turned to him. "Look no disrespect, I love Dove like a play cousin, but you need to keep rhyming. I know you got the same dreams I've got and you can't afford to waste time. If Dynamite, Flame or Raindance came to me talking like that, I'd keep rhyming without them. They would expect that and respect that. Dove has the family not you, I think he will understand. It'll be a mistake to procrastinate."

"Yeah, you're right. Can you turn in this exit?" Hawk asked.

FOG dropped Hawk off at his building. Edgar "Hawk" Dewitt entered, placed his keys on the coffee table and turned on the lamp near the couch. He turned on Common Sense's "Resurrection," sat on the couch and reflected on his career so far. He thought about how Hawk and Dove rocked shows and different events, like the rhythm and poetry show at Howard, the Abstract Griot, and the 9:30 Club He thought of how Dove always took control on stage and how he booked all of the shows that they performed. Maybe going solo wouldn't be such a bad idea. Hawk pulled out the current copy of the *D.C. City Reader* and looked in the classified section under music.

Sunday morning at the Prince George's Hospital Center, Lawrence "Dove" Hall and his wife Victoria were at the hospital waiting to speak to Julia's doctor. Dr. Shepard approached them

"Good morning Mr. and Mrs. Hall, we gave Julia Pneumovex to control the infection and medication to relieve the pain but she still has a fever. The medication helped her to sleep, we would like to keep her until she's feeling better."

"Thank you Dr. Shepard." Dove shook his hand.

"Can we see her?" Victoria asked.

"You sure can." Dr. Shepard smiled.

When Dove and Victoria got to Julia's room she was asleep. Dove took Victoria's hand. "She'll be fine, we must have faith."

"I know but I wish I could do more." Victoria whispered.

"So do I baby." They both kissed her on the cheek and left the room.

"Are you hungry?" Dove asked Victoria.

"I'm starving." She rubbed her empty stomach.

"Let's go down to The Abstract Griot for brunch, The Tucker Mills Quartet plays live jazz there every Sunday morning."

"Lawrence I don't feel like going downtown, let's go up the street to Denny's instead."

"Okay honey." Dove said disappointed, he hated Denny's.

That night at The Abstract Griot, Mood, Hawk, Dynamite, Paradise and FOG sat in a booth while Toni was reading her poetry on stage.

"How is Dove doing?" Paradise looked directly at Hawk.

"I don't know, I tried calling his house but I didn't get an answer." Hawk said putting a packet of sugar into his iced tea.

"Maybe he spent the day at the hospital." Dynamite said.

"I'll see him tomorrow, my building's on his route." Mood said.

"Tell him we've all been praying for him and his family Mood." FOG said.

Kenny came out of the kitchen with their dinner orders. "Let's see, baked chicken with macaroni and cheese."

"That's me." FOG licked his lips.

"Mood, you had the Hoppin' John. Dynamite, the ham and cheese on toast was yours and you get a free ice tea with that."

"Thanks Kenny." Dynamite reached for the mayo.

"Hawk here's the pork chops with the mashed potatoes. Paradise, you had the red beans and rice."

"Thanks Kenny, this all looks really good." Paradise said.

"Thanks Paradise. Dynamite, I need to talk to you when you get some time."

"No problem." Dynamite said while munching on his sandwich.

"Hey Mood, where's Sabrina? I'm surprised she's not attached to your arm tonight." Paradise said.

"She and her friend Melanie went to Dave and Buster's, Melanie needed a study break." Mood said.

"And you didn't go?" Hawk asked.

"I haven't missed Sunday night poetry in three years." Mood said proudly. "What about your girls Paradise?"

Flame went to see that movie *Rhyme and Reason* and Dana's preparing a math quiz to test her class tomorrow."

"I really wasn't feeling that movie." Hawk said.

"But you must admit it was much better than *The Show*." Dynamite said.

"Yo! That RZA video they played before the movie began was tight though." FOG said.

"True," Paradise said. "I thought that new Wu-Tang album would be out by now."

"It got pushed back until this summer." FOG said. Just then Toni introduced Mood.

"Excuse me." Mood said as he got up and headed over to the stage.

Across the ocean, a lifetime away
I sit on the sands of foreign shores
Envisioning a time when I can see you again
When we won't be forced apart due to another war
We shared every full moon together by the beach
And although we're apart
We still share every full moon together by the beach.
I close my eyes and see you on the other side of the ocean
Sitting on the sand
The glow of the moon reflecting off the tear
That streams down your cheek
As I sit on the sands of foreign shores
I imagine walking across the ocean

Where you will be waiting
Where your beauty will inspire me to make love to you
Against the rocks while overlooking sand castles
Someday, I will make this dream come true
As I place this red rose in a bottle
And throw it into the ocean, hoping it will reach you
Across the ocean, a lifetime away.

Applause filled The Abstract Griot as Mood opened his eyes. "Thanks." Mood said as he exited the stage, he hugged Toni and went back to the table.

"That's the most beautiful poem I ever heard you recite." Paradise said.

"It's based on a true story." Mood said.

"That joint almost put a tear to my eyes." FOG said.

"Look, even Moms came out of the kitchen to hear you." Hawk said.

Kenny came to the table. "Wow." Was all he could say.

"Thanks." Mood said modestly.

Kenny turned to Dynamite. "Could you come with me?" They walked outside into the cool spring evening and they went around the corner. On the brick wall next to the window was blue spray painted lettering "COOL DISS GO SAM."

"I knew I couldn't keep this wall graffiti free forever." Kenny said.

"Yeah his tag is all over D.C., I've even seen it as far up north as Philly." Dynamite lit a cigarette.

"I want to hire you to paint a mural right here, I will pay for everything you need, you're the artist. You can paint whatever you want as long as it's not offensive. Cool Diss Go Sam got me once, he won't get me again."

"No problem, but why did you ask me?" Dynamite asked while observing the wall.

"Because your work is incredible that's why, you graduated top of your class at the Corcoran School of Art."

"I'll do it, I'll work on some ideas and get the ball rolling right away."

"Alright." Kenny exclaimed as he gave Dynamite a pound. "I have to make some calls."

Monday morning at 7:00 Lawrence "Dove" Hall lazily walked into the Brentwood Post Office, one of the largest postal facilities in the city. After he clocked in, he walked over to his work case and observed the eight trays of letters, the tubs of magazines and the big hamper of parcels and priority packages.

"Damn! This is gonna be a long day." He said as he reached into his backpack for his Walkman. While reaching into his bag he discovered that he still had the Antigravity demo that Flame gave him. "I'd better make sure those cats at Power records check this out." He thought facing his case, just then Dove felt a tap on his shoulder.

"Hey Jake, what's new?" Jake Matthews was a veteran carrier of twenty years and trained Dove during his first week as a carrier.

"That girl Roxanne has been around here looking for you already." Jake said.

"Damn, doesn't she know I'm married?"

"Apparently she doesn't care, so how was your weekend?"

"Not too good, Julia's in the hospital again."

"What did the doctor say?" Jake asked.

"She's recovering slowly, I hope she'll be home soon." Dove said.

"Well I'll be praying for her." Jake said.

"Here comes the supervisor." Dove watched Ms. Gates walk to where the two men stood.

"Did you gentleman come here to work or to socialize?" She said.

Jake went back to his case while Dove put on his headphones and began putting the mail in his case. At 10:00, Dove received a page from his wife, he went to call on the lobby payphone.

"Crestar Bank, this is Victoria."

"Good morning honey, How are you feeling?" Dove asked.

"I'm okay, what about you?"

"I'm a little tired, every time Julia's in the hospital I have difficulty sleeping." Dove yawned.

"Hopefully she'll be home soon, I'm planning on going by the hospital on my lunch hour. Will you be getting off on time tonight?"

"I don't think so." He said with disappointed tone. "The mail's real heavy, but that's a typical Monday here."

"O.K. I have to go, I have customers."

"Alright," Said Dove. "I love you."

"I love you too baby." Victoria hung up the phone.

At 12:30 Dove had pulled down of all his mail, placed it on his cart and wheeled it to the platform where his mail truck was parked. He began to load his mail into his vehicle when Ms. Gates came to the platform with a clipboard in her hand.

"Mr. Hall, I need you to do a one hour bump for me. Rogers is on all day overtime."

"Ms. Gates, I have enough mail to deliver and my little girl is in the hospital, I have to go see her."

Ms. Gates cut him off. "Listen I sympathize with your situation but I have no choice. You are a part time flex and I can work you from four to twelve hours. It's only an hour, Now please follow my instructions." And she walked away.

Dove angrily walked back inside, loaded the extra mail and drove away.

Hawk walked into the Martin Luther King Library at 1:00, He was dressed in a black Kangol, beige khakis and a red button down Polo shirt.

"Good afternoon Clive." Hawk said as he passed the guard in the lobby.

"Hi Edgar, how was your weekend?"

66

"It was cool." He said. He never mentioned his business to Clive because Clive would spread it all over the library. Hawk took the elevator to the third floor, walked into the break room and reached for some change in his pocket. He purchased a bottle of apple juice and a bag of potato chips. He walked to the music section where he worked and sat behind the desk. After his snack he looked around and began his job. He wheeled a cart around, picked up the books from the table and began to reshelf them. "That didn't take long." He thought as he sat behind his desk. He noticed that mostly homeless people and senior citizens filled the music section. "The library's not full of activity until the kids get out of school." He thought as he pulled out his composition notebook and started writing rhymes. During the afternoon people would approach him for information about certain jazz records that were hard to find. Hawk knew music and was glad that his boss gave him the morning off so that he could run errands with his father and pick up some beats from Montel, a producer with whom he and Dove occasionally worked. A tall gentleman wearing a nylon Nike sweat suit and a pair of Stan Smith's Adidas approached Hawk.

"Excuse me, Can you help me? I was wondering if you had EPMD's Unfinished Business."

Hawk looked up from his notebook and said. "The only EPMD album we have is Strictly Business, we don't have an elaborate hip-hop collection here. It's mostly jazz, classical and rock and roll."

"Oh," He noticed Hawk's rhyme filled notebook. "Are you a rapper?"

"Yeah." Hawk said.

"My name is Rashad Morrison and I manage acts in the area. Do you perform regularly?"

"I did with my partner but now I'm doing my own thing."

"Well here's my card, call me if you need a manager, I can get you some exposure."

"Thanks." Hawk looked at the card it read "Top Grade Management, Rashad Morrison." "I'll do that." He put the card into his backpack. "My name is Edgar Dewitt, they call me 'Hawk'."

"Well I hope to hear from you soon Hawk."

"I'm gonna be late." Dove spoke into the phone on Mood's desk.

"Are you still going to be able to see Julia? She's been asking for you." Victoria said.

"I know, I'm definitely going after work. How is she feeling?"

"The doctor just gave her some antibiotics to control the infection and some medication to keep her blood from becoming too thick. He said she's doing well, he thinks she'll be able to come home by the end of the week."

"That's good, look I can't keep this line tied up, I have to go."

"Alright Lawrence, I love you."

"I love you too, I'll call you when I get done Bye." After Dove got off of the phone Mood returned to the desk.

"So how's the family?" Mood asked.

"Well Victoria just left the hospital, she said they predict Julia will be home by the end of the week."

"That's good news. How are you doing?" Mood asked.

"I'm trying to deal with it, It hasn't hit me yet like it has hit Victoria. I have to chill with rhyming for a second in order to take care of my fam. I feel bad because I left Hawk in a lurch." Dove said.

"Your family is your priority, we'll be there when you decide to bless us with your presence. In the mean time I'll keep you informed."

"Thanks Mood. How are you and Sabrina?"

"Smooth as butter brother, we're supposed to be going to see that movie *Love Jones* tonight." Mood smiled. "People have been telling me that it's a good movie, it's supposed to change the direction of black cinema." Dove said.

"I'll let you know, maybe you and Victoria can see it."

"Give me your review tomorrow." Dove said as he hugged Mood and began to leave.

A lady in the lobby watched them hug and said. "It's good to know that some brothers are still out there hugging each other instead of killing each other." She said as she waited for the elevator.

By 4:30 the library was very busy. Hawk worked at the checkout counter on the first floor. School children were all over the place, some were studying, while some boys were going from floor to floor while trying to get phone numbers. One little boy in particular reminded Hawk of himself when he was young. His name is Mario and he was talking to every girl wearing a Catholic school uniform. He looked up at Hawk and gave him a thumb's up every time he got a girl's phone number. Hawk laughed and looked up as he saw Dana walk in. "Dana!" He called.

Looking beautiful in a navy blue pantsuit, she gazed at him and smiled as she made her way over to the checkout counter.

"Hey Hawk, I thought you worked upstairs in the music department."

"I do but someone called in sick so they asked me to come work down here, I think it has something to do with me getting caught writing rhymes. What are you doing here?"

"I asked one of my students to meet me here so that I can tutor him in history, I chose the library because of the comfortable atmosphere."

"I heard about what that teacher did, if that was my little girl I don't know what I would've done." Hawk said.

"I know, I wish I could go to that school where he teaches and ring his neck but I have to be strong. Paradise told me about Dove's little girl. How is she feeling?"

"I don't know, he hasn't returned my calls, I'm gonna try again tonight."

"Give him my love." Dana said looking around. "Here

comes my kid now."

Mario walked towards the desk. "Hi Mario, Are you ready to study?"

"Yes Ms. Conners." Mario said with an angelic smile.

"Let's go upstairs. Hawk, I'll see you later." As they walked away Mario turned to Hawk, smiled and gave him a thumbs up.

"That little muthafucka." Hawk thought and laughed.

Dove arrived at the hospital and checked his watch. "7:30. Damn I wish I could've gotten here sooner." He thought when he walked into Julia's room Victoria sat in a chair by Julia's bed reading *Cinderella*. Victoria looked up and said. "Look who's here honey."

Julia turned to look and said. "Daddy!" She held her arms out for a big hug. "Daddy, I missed you."

"I missed you too, How are you baby girl?"

"I'm okay Daddy, I'm ready to go home."

"You have to get better first then you'll be home real soon Okay?"

"Okay Daddy." She said sadly. After Victoria finished the story, the three of them watched Pocahontas until it was time for her to go to sleep.

"I'm sleepy Daddy, Mommy will you say my prayers with me?"

"Sure baby."

The three of them got on their knees beside the bed and Julia began. "Now I lay me down to sleep. I pray the Lord my soul to keep. If I should die before I wake I pray the Lord my soul to take. God bless Mommy, Daddy, Hawk and Mr. Bear, and please let me get better soon. Amen."

"Amen, that was very good honey." Dove said as he tucked her in.

"Don't worry Daddy I'm gonna be a big girl." Julia said.

"That's my big girl, I love you." He hugged her tight.

"I love you too Daddy goodnight."

She drifted off to sleep minutes later, Dove and Victoria got up to leave. When they got home Victoria kicked off her shoes and went up to the bedroom, where she laid down across the bed. Dove came in behind her sat on the bed, and rubbed her back.

"She's going to be just fine." Dove said trying to convince himself.

"I know but it just keeps getting harder and harder to leave her there, we ruined her life before she had a chance to live it. She got sickle cell because of the two of us." She began to cry.

"You can't blame us for that," Dove said. "We also gave that girl life, her smile and her laugh. She also a very strong little girl." He looked directly into her eyes, wiped her tears and said. "She gets that strength from you." She hugged him and got dressed for bed. Dove went to the bathroom and began to undress. "Finally." He thought while taking off his uniform. He turned on the radio and jumped into the shower. As he reached for the soap one of Julia's Little Mermaid toys sat on the side of the tub. He suddenly remembered the last time that he gave her a bath and they played with the Little Mermaid toy. As he reminisced, tears rolled down the side of his face as he fell to his knees in the tub and cried as the water rained all around him.

Thursday morning at 10:00, Hawk walked up 14th Street until he got to the corner of 14th and R Streets. A sign on the window read. "Top Grade Management." From the window he could see a woman with a new hairdo who worked behind the front desk. "At least it's not an apartment." He thought. He walked through one door and waited for the buzz that would allow him to enter the second door. After he was buzzed in he approached the front desk. "May I help you?" The receptionist asked.

"Yes I have an appointment with Mr. Morrison, my name is Hawk."

"Have a seat please." She popped her chewing gum

71

and picked up her phone.

"Rashad, there's a gentleman named Hawk here to see you. Uh huh, uh huh." She hung up the phone. "He'll be right with you."

A few minutes later Rashad came out to meet Hawk. "Hey Hawk, how are you?" He extended his hand and Hawk shook it.

"I've been alright." Hawk said.

"Good come with me to my office. Sally take messages for me, I'm in a meeting."

"Yes Rashad." She popped her gum.

Hawk looked around his office and noticed pictures of all of Rashad's clients, many of whom had gone on to have success.

"Have a seat Hawk."

Hawk sat down in the chair while Rashad sat down behind the desk. "Hold on." Hawk reached into his backpack and pulled out EPMD's *Unfinished Business* on cassette. "I thought you might want to borrow this, you can give it back when you're done with it. Here's a sample of some of my work."

Hawk handed him a tape with two songs that he had worked on with Montel. Rashad placed the tape in his tape deck and began to listen to it. While the tape played Rashad shook his head to the beat while Hawk silently mouthed the words.

After Rashad heard the tape he said. "Wow that's pretty good." He opened up his schedule book and said. "Look Hawk, there's an audition for the Insomnia Talent Show this Saturday at 2:00. Are you interested in auditioning?"

"Yeah that would be cool."

"Alright, Let me make a phone call."

"Let me ask you something," Hawk began. "How do I pay you?"

"Well at Top Grade Management, we only ask for twenty percent of any show we set up for you. Since this is an audition let's just label this a trial run."

"Alright." Hawk said.

"Good, I'll call you Saturday morning with directions to the talent show."

Hawk got up to leave and Rashad walked him to the front door. "Thank you for the opportunity." Hawk put on his Walkman and left.

"You're welcome and thank you for the EPMD tape." He said as Hawk walked down the hall.

Later that evening at The Abstract Griot, Raindance sat at a table eating candy yams when Hawk walked in and sat down.

"Hey Raindance, what's new?"

"Nothing much, I'm just chillin' and enjoying the music."

The music was coming from Spider Web, a jazz band well known in the D.C. area.

"Guess what? I'm auditioning for the Insomnia Talent Show on Saturday."

"How did you land that? We've been trying to get in that audition all week, it's real exclusive."

"Well I just got down with Top Grade Management, Rashad is the man in charge, he said he'd hook it up. Can you come to the audition with me?" Hawk asked.

"That's possible, call me and we'll meet you there."

Kenny came to the table and said. "What's up Hawk? Have you heard from Dove?"

"I left messages on his machine, He still hasn't returned any of my calls."

"Are you going to tell him about Saturday?" Raindance asked.

"Well I thought about it, if I pass the auditions I was gonna invite him to the show. I don't want him to think I'm playahating" Hawk said.

"I hope his little girl is doing okay." Kenny said concerned.

"I hoped he would have at least called me, we've been best friends since high school. I hope everything's well." Hawk looked at his watch and said. "I've got to run, I have to meet my parents for dinner."

"Peace." Kenny said.

"Yeah, peace out." Raindance said.

As Hawk left Paradise walked in. Her baby locks poked out of her head. "Hey Hawk what's your hurry? It's still early."

"I've got a previous engagement, I can't stay." He said.

"Who's inside?"

"Kenny and Raindance." He said as he proceeded over to 7th street to the Shaw/Howard U. Metro.

On Friday afternoon, Dove and Victoria got Julia ready to go home. Dove packed her things and got all of her flowers and toys together while Victoria dressed her.

Dr. Shepard walked in. "Well look who's leaving me today."

"Dr. Shepard, I'm going home today." Julia beamed.

"I know, How are you feeling?" He asked her while crouching to make eye contact.

"I feel a lot better." She said as she reached over to hug him.

"I'm glad," He said. "But can Mr. Bear stay?" He asked with a big smile.

"No way, Mr. Bear doesn't like the hospital."

"Okay I understand." He laughed and stood up. "Mr. and Mrs. Hall, may I see you in the hall?"

The three of them walked into the hall while Julia played with Mr. Bear. In the hall they sat on the couch, Dr. Shepard said. "I know you're glad to finally get Julia home."

"True." Dove said.

"Yeah it's been hard to sleep at night." Victoria said.

"I understand, I have two little ones at home myself. Now here is a prescription for some penicillin. Please make sure she's given penicillin every day, you should feel her

74

spleen regularly for enlargement. When a spleen becomes enlarged, it has trapped a large amount of circulating blood cells. If that happens, call 911 immediately. Make sure she gets plenty of folic acid, zinc, vitamin and cynate in her diet."

"What's cynate?" Dove asked.

"Cynate is a non toxic relative to the chemical cyanide. It can be found in radishes, carrots, cabbage and kidney beans." He handed them a nutrition list. "She needs to eat smaller portions in several meals throughout the day. She also has an appointment to see me again on Tuesday morning at 9:00." Dr. Shepard said as he stood up. Dove and Victoria stood up too. Dove shook his hand and Dr. Shepard left to make his rounds.

On the way home they stopped at the drugstore to have the prescription filled and to the supermarket to pick up groceries. When they got home Dove cooked dinner and all of them sat at the kitchen table and held hands while Julia said the grace. Dove looked over at his family and thought to himself. "Finally we are one again, Thank you Lord."

On Saturday afternoon, Hawk anxiously waited in line for the Insomnia Talent Auditions at the Ascot. He read the contents of the folder that Rashad had given to him. The folder contained a flier of the finals, which showed the first prize of $300 dollars, rules for the auditions and the finals were also enclosed. The rules for the auditions stated that each performer would have three minutes to display her or his talent. Hawk practiced all night to ensure that three minutes was all that he would need to rock the crowd. They opened the doors to the Ascot at 2:30 on the nose. Hawk walked in, signed in and sat down next to a singing group consisting of three women, all dressed alike, who practiced their harmonies. Hawk was impressed.

"Y'all sound really good," He said. "Good luck on the auditions."

"Thank you." Said the girl sitting closest to him. "Are

you a rapper?"

"Yeah, my name is Hawk." He extended his hand to meet her handshake.

"My name is Kiesha, this is Shauna, and Tootie. Together we're Phenomenon." Tootie and Shauna both waved.

"I'm kinda nervous, this is my first solo show. I hope I make this audition." Hawk said.

"We've been together for four years, we finally decided to stop procrastinating and go for it." Kiesha said.

A gentleman came up to the microphone. "Good afternoon, welcome to the third annual Insomnia Talent Show preliminaries. You have three minutes to showcase your talent. Over here to my left is our panel of judges, they will be judging you based on your performance, stage presence and of course talent. Those of you who make the finals will be required to sell tickets to the event. Tickets are ten dollars each. The purpose of this event is to give many of you exposure, Our final showcase will have many representatives from Def Jam, Motown and Bad Boy records. Good luck to all of you."

He looked down his list of performers. "Our first act is Most Wanted."

Three camouflage clad brothers got on stage. While their track played they belted out rhymes about their favorite pastime: smoking weed. The hook was "Puff it up, puff it up, puff it up."

Hawk looked around the club but didn't recognize anyone there. After Most Wanted left the stage, a jazz group called Meltdown performed a rendition of Mo' Better Blues. Phenomenon went on next and performed Minnie Ripperton's "Inside My Love." acapella. Their performance received a standing ovation.

"You ladies were remarkable." Hawk said when they sat down.

"Thanks." Keisha smiled.

"We appreciate that." Tootie said.

It was another hour before Hawk went on. "Next up is Hawk."

"It's about time." He handed the guy at the tape deck a cued instrumental track that Montel hooked up, then went onto the stage. He was nervous about his first solo performance but he kept his composure.

"What's up everybody, How y'all feelin'?"

"Alright. "the crowd responded.

"My name is Hawk, the song I'm gonna perform is called 'For the Moment'."

The music started and Hawk took off lyrically. Verse one told the tale of how men will tell you how much they love you until they make love, and how those feelings last only for the moment. Verse two told how a rapper found fame, but his fame lasted for the moment because he sacrificed his music for the dollar. Full of energy and confidence he moved from one side of the stage to the other. He looked out at the crowd and knew he had them.

After his song and the applause he returned to where the ladies of Phenomenon sat. Kiesha said. "You were really good, I thought you said you were nervous."

"I was, Did it show?"

"Not at all, the way you moved from one side of the stage to the other was wonderful."

"Well that's because I had to go to the bathroom." He joked.

The ladies laughed. "You're crazy Hawk."

At 5:00 the last act went on. It was rap act called Folklore. The group consisted of one girl, two guys and a DJ. After their performance, there was a thirty minutes of waiting while the judges were picking out the finalists.

The announcer approached the stage. "Thanks for your patience, We'd like to thank all of you for coming out to share your talents, the judges had a difficult time but here are your finalists: Meltdown, Most Wanted, Phenomenon, Bad Brew, Everclear, Vision, Mad Dog, and Hawk."

"Yahoo." He thought.

"The Insomnia talent competition will take place next Saturday right here at the Ascot, have a good evening. Finalists, please see me tonight so that I can give the details to you."

"Congratulations Hawk, now we're competitors." Kiesha smiled.

"But it's three to one, What's up with that?"

"Well here's my number, call me and let me know if you're ready for some one on one."

Hawk smiled as the ladies left and sang. "One on One" by Hall and Oates.

On Monday, Mood sat at his desk when Dove walked in. "Hey What's up Mood?"

"Hey what's up Dove, I didn't see you walk in."

"You look like you have a lot on your mind. What's up?"

"That fool George is playahatin'. He's still pissed off because Sabrina and I are dating, he called my concierge company and told them that he's been getting complaints about me and asked if I could be replaced."

"Word?"

"Yeah and now one of my bosses is coming over to evaluate me this afternoon."

"Damn that's cold, It'll be fine though just explain the situation to them."

"Oh I will, I'm also gonna talk to Mr. Blake about it. Have you talked to Hawk yet?" Mood asked while putting his newspaper away.

"No but I've been meaning to call. Why?"

"Because he came by The Abstract Griot last night happier than a Disney movie. He auditioned for a show on Saturday and made the finals, he said the show was this coming Saturday. I'm surprised he didn't tell you, you two are best friends."

"He has been calling and leaving messages, Victoria talked to him once when he called. I just haven't returned his phone calls, you know how it is when you're busy."

"Yeah I know." Mood said. "Maybe you should go over to the library and see what's up with him."

"I think I'll do that." Dove said.

Suddenly Mood's attention shifted when his boss Mary Taylor walked in. "I gotta go, here comes my boss."

"Good luck." Dove said.

"Thanks, I'm going to need it."

Dove finished his route and looked at his watch at 4:45. He drove his mail truck to the Martin Luther King Library and parked on 9th and G Streets. He walked in and went to the music section. Dove looked around and saw Hawk putting books on the shelves. "Hey Mr. Dewitt. What's new?"

Hawk turned around and was surprised to see Dove standing there. He dropped the book that he had in his hand onto the cart, walked over and hugged his friend.

"Do you know who you sounded like just now?" Hawk smiled.

Dove answered. "Yeah Mr. Duncan when he caught you in the bathroom at Ellington with Marla Martin."

"Word." They both laughed.

"So how's Julia doing? Victoria said she was better last time I talked to her."

"She's doing alright, getting stronger every day, she came home on Friday." Dove said.

"That's good."

"I meant to call you, I just heard about your audition. How did you hear about the audition?"

"I hooked up with Top Grade Management, they got me the audition."

"Word! I'm glad you're staying active." Dove tried to hide his jealousy.

"Well you're coming aren't you? I'm gonna need you there."

"No doubt, When is it?" Dove's face lit up.

"This coming Saturday at the Ascot." Hawk said.

"I'll be there." The alarm on his watch went off. "Look I've got to go, I'll see you later."

"Peace man and don't be a stranger." Hawk said.

When Dove got home that evening, Victoria was cooking dinner and Julia was helping. Dove kissed Victoria and Julia and then went to the bedroom where he changed into a pair of baggy gray sweat pants and a black WSOL tee shirt. They all sat at the table, said grace and began to eat.

"So how was your day today honey?" Victoria asked Dove.

"It was fine, I had a good day. I'm glad it's getting hot again."

"I don't understand how you can work in all that heat."

"I'd rather have the heat at boiler room hot than have to trudge through all the winter's snow. How about your day?"

"It was really good, they told me I'm up for a promotion to branch management."

"That's good sweetheart, Congratulations."

"Thank you. You see Julia, if you work hard good things happen to you." Julia shook her head as she stuck a fork full of green beans into her mouth.

"Guess who I saw today?"

"Who Daddy?" Julia asked.

"I saw Hawk." Dove said.

"How's he doing?" Victoria asked.

"He's doing fine, he auditioned for a show last Saturday and made the finals. He needs me to rhyme with him."

"When is the show?" Victoria asked between bites of her potatoes.

"This Saturday at the Ascot."

"You know this Saturday is the same evening as the Crestar banquet dinner."

"I thought that was next Saturday." Dove said slapping his forehead with his hand. Julia imitated him.

"No dear, if you had been listening, you would have known it was this Saturday."

"I do listen to you." Dove slightly raised his voice.

"I thought you said you were going to stop all this hanging out."

"In case you haven't noticed I have stopped hanging out all the time, It's just one show." He put his fork down.

"That's right," She countered. "It's always just one show, then another and another."

They stopped arguing when they realized that Julia was in the room with them. "We'll continue this conversation later."

After dinner, Dove and Julia watched television in the basement while Victoria updated her resume on the computer. When it was Julia's bedtime, they both helped her get dressed for bed. Victoria felt for spleen enlargement while Julia put her nightshirt on.

"Mommy, why are you and Daddy fighting?"

"We are not fighting dear, we're just having a talk about something we don't see eye to eye on, like a debate."

"Oh." Julia said as she climbed into bed. "Can we read *Jack and the Beanstalk*?"

They read the story together and they said their prayers. Before Victoria turned off her light Julia said. "I hope you win the debate Mommy, us girls got to stick together."

Victoria laughed and said. "Good night baby, I love you."

"I love you too."

When Victoria went into the bedroom, Dove was lying in bed reading *The Source*. Victoria changed into a pink teddy and slid under the covers next to her husband. She broke the silence by saying. "I just don't understand, you have a good job, a beautiful home, and a family who loves you. You've done more at less than thirty years of age than most do at forty. Why is that not enough for you?"

"All I want to do is follow my dreams."

"You don't think you're gonna get some type of record

deal do you?" Victoria rolled her eyes.

"All I want to do is follow my dreams. The post office is a place where dreams are shackled down by overtime, you'd be surprised at how many wannabes are working down there. I don't want to be like that, it ain't even about a record deal. It's that feeling that I get when I'm rhyming and moving the crowd, it's like feeding a hunger."

"I understand that but this dinner is very important, there will be important people there. It could even help me get that promotion, I suggest that you choose what's important to you." Victoria said as she turned over to go to sleep.

Dove checked the alarm, turned out the light and stared at the ceiling until he fell asleep.

All week after work Dove took advantage of staying at home by mowing the lawn, cleaning the gutters and working on his "honey do" list. Hawk spent the week working on tracks with FOG, practicing for the show and selling tickets to those who could afford the $10 cover charge. On Friday Dove loaded his mail into his truck and stopped off at the Martin Luther King library. Hawk worked at the checkout counter when Dove walked in wearing his post office shorts.

"Look who's showing some leg!" Hawk whistled at Dove.

"Shut up fool." Dove joked. They both laughed.

"What's up with tomorrow?"

"Well the show starts at four and I'm slated to go on third."

"Word! That'll work, I'm supposed to go to some stupid dinner that Vicki's job is throwing but that's not until eight." Dove said. "We'll be done in plenty of time."

"Why don't you bring her along?" Hawk asked. "It's a comfortable atmosphere."

"I was planning on coming straight from work, besides how many of our shows has she attended in the past? She's been to The Abstract Griot only once."

"That's true." Hawk said thinking back.

Dove looked up at the clock. "I'd better get started, I have to go to Today's Man and pick up a tie and some new shoes."

"Eee-yew." Hawk said. "Better you than me."

"I know." Dove said. After work Dove met Victoria and Julia at Today's Man. He picked out a pair of wingtip shoes that were on sale while Victoria picked out a tie that worked well with his black suit at home. As they drove home Dove said. "Sweetheart the show starts at four and I can leave early enough to attend the dinner."

"That's great baby but you need to be home by seven so we can leave by 7:30."

Dove looked straight ahead while driving.

"Okay baby." He said not really paying attention.

On Saturday at 3:00 there was a long line outside of the Ascot for the Insomnia Talent Showcase. Dove drove around for ten minutes before he found a parking space. He walked towards the Ascot and was dressed in a black CK long sleeve tee shirt, a pair of black baggy Levi's SilverTab jeans, a light beige jacket and a pair of sand-colored Timberlands. He walked across the street and towards the end of the line.

"Dove! Hey Dove!"

He turned and saw Paradise dressed in a blue denim shirt, a pair of black cotton pants and a black leather jacket.

"What's up Paradise?" He hugged her. "I haven't seen you since..."

"Since the night your daughter got sick, so how is she doing?"

"She's doing a lot better now, what have you been up to?"

"Well I've been submitting my writing to *Washingtonian* magazine and to the *Post*. I'm trying to generate more money so I can pay the rent. I haven't heard anything yet, but I'm thinking positive."

"Wow there's no stopping you is there?" Dove said

impressed.

"I'm here tonight covering this story for the *D.C. City Reader*."

"Make your moves girl," He paused and said. "I can't wait to get on stage."

Paradise looked confused. "What do you mean?"

"Well he told me he needs me here, I figured we'd do *Broken Glass*, that's our best song."

When they got to the door Dove said. "Hey my name is Dove, I should be on the list under Hawk and Dove."

"I see Hawk but no Dove, now pay ten dollars or move out of the way."

"What? Who do you think you're talkin' to like that?"

Paradise jumped in. "Hold on, I'm Evelyn Patterson and I'm with the *D.C. City Reader*, I should be on the list."

"Yes, you're okay."

"He's with me, he's my photographer." Paradise shoved her 35 millimeter camera into his hands. "Yeah." He lifted the camera up to show him.

"Okay go ahead inside."

"Thanks Paradise that brother was tripping, I was about to get loud."

"Yeah, I saw that coming."

They walked in and looked around, they spotted Hawk at the bar. He was talking to a woman in a black mini dress.

"Yo Hawk!" Hawk wore a long sleeved green shirt and Polo blue jeans, he had a drink in his hand and he hugged Dove and Paradise.

"This is Keisha, she sings in a group called Phenomenon. Wait until you hear them sing, they're the bomb. Keisha this is Dove."

"Hi Dove, I've heard a lot about you." Keisha shook Dove's hand.

"It's nice to meet you."

"And that's Paradise, she's our home girl and she writes for the *D.C. City Reader*." Hawk said.

"How are you?" Then she continued to write on her

notepad.

"So how long have you been here?" Dove asked Hawk.

"Well, all performers had to be here earlier for a sound check."

"You should have told me, I would've been here earlier," Dove said. "Since we haven't practiced all week, I figured we could do *Broken Glass*. We don't need to practice to do that joint."

Hawk was confused. "What are you talking about?"

"I'm talking about our performance."

"Our performance?" Suddenly it became clear to Hawk. "Dove, I think we need to have a talk. Will you ladies excuse us?"

Hawk led Dove to the men's room "Dove I'm really glad you came out, but there's something you should know."

"What's wrong?" Dove asked.

"I planned on performing solo."

"What do you mean? I thought you needed me here tonight."

"I do need you here, I need you here for support. I need you right here so if I get nervous I could look up and see my best friend, I'm sorry if you misunderstood."

Dove held back his hurt and smiled. "It's cool." He said and gave his friend a hug.

"Are you in a position to return to hip-hop?" Hawk asked.

"Well truthfully no."

They walked back into the now crowded Ascot just as the announcer introduced the first act. Hawk and Dove sat at a circular table with Paradise.

The show began and the first act was Most Wanted. Most Wanted got on stage and started screaming. "You owe me!" *You Owe Me* was the title of their song about owing the black man for all of the hardships black people went through. The second act was Phenomenon.

When the ladies passed the table Hawk said. "Good

luck, knock 'em dead."

Keisha smiled.

Hawk said to Dove and Paradise. "Wait until you hear them."

"I better take a picture." Paradise said.

Dove remained silent.

Phenomenon ripped up the stage with their rendition of Tonya Blount's *Through the Rain*. Keisha sang lead while Shauna and Tootie sang background. They left the stage to a standing ovation. When Keisha left the stage she hugged Hawk and said. "You're next, good luck."

"I'm gonna need it since I'm performing behind you."

"You'll be fine." She said.

The announcer introduced Hawk. Hawk handed his backpack to Dove and said to them. "Wish me luck."

"Good luck." Paradise said.

Dove was silent.

Hawk got on stage and began to freestyle He freestyled about the "Queens" in the audience until his music came on. A bouncy track radiated through the Ascot and Hawk performed a song called *Similies like these*." He rhymed in an abstract style and the audience was bouncing up and down. Dove watched how Hawk handled himself on the stage, then he observed the crowd's reaction and although he was impressed he couldn't hide his jealousy. He handed Hawk's backpack to Paradise, grabbed his jacket and got up to leave without saying goodbye. Hawk watched him from the stage and looked at Paradise. Paradise shrugged her shoulders and mouthed the words. "I don't know." He continued to rhyme as he watched Dove walk out of the door.

When Dove got outside rain poured down from the sky. "This is just perfect." he thought as he ran across the street to his car. He drove home in silence feeling very depressed. When he got home Victoria's sister, Lydia and Julia were playing with Julia's blocks.

"Hi Lawrence."

Lydia was the most bubbly of Victoria's two sisters,

she was also the youngest. She looked like Victoria except her face was slimmer.

"Hey Lydia, what's new?"

"Nothing much, I'm babysitting tonight. We've got ice cream, popcorn, Cinderella and Bambi."

"Sounds like a fun night," Dove said. "Where's Victoria?"

"She went to the store to buy some stockings. Are you okay?"

"Just wonderful," Dove said sarcastically. "I'm going to take a shower and get ready."

"Daddy."

"Yes baby?"

"I learned how to write my name in cursive."

"That's very good honey, I'll be right back." Dove took a shower and put on his black suit, a white shirt and his new pair of shoes.

Victoria walked in the bedroom. "Hey sweetie." Victoria kissed him, sat on the bed and put on her stockings. "How was the show?"

"It was a waste of time," He said in a low tone. "I didn't stay."

"Why not?" She asked.

"I don't want to talk about it."

"Alright." She put her shoes back on.

They went downstairs. Lydia and Julia were playing Tetris on the Sony PlayStation. "We're leaving now," Victoria said. "If you need me just call Lawrence's pager."

They got in the car. Victoria drove and talked but Dove wasn't listening.

Knowing her husband Victoria said. "Listen if you're going to be like this all night we can turn around and go home right now."

Dove got upset. "Fine." He said raising his voice. "I didn't want to be around those fake assholes you work with anyway."

"Listen." She said as she stopped at a red light. "I don't

know what your problem is but you will not disrespect me."

"Whatever." He said.

"That's it." She said she turned the car around and headed back home.

Once they got home Dove walked in, slammed the door and went into the bedroom. Victoria walked in frowning. Lydia came up from the basement. "What happened? Did he forget something?"

"No he's PMSing! Something's bothering him and he doesn't want to talk about it, I bet it has something to do with Hawk. Anyway he's not ruining my evening, put your shoes on I'm taking you and Julia with me."

"Okay, I have to run home and change." Lydia hugged her and said. "Don't worry, he'll break out of his shell soon enough."

"I hope so." Victoria said with tears welling up in her eyes. She went downstairs to get Julia.

Victoria got Julia dressed and went to the bedroom. "I'm leaving and I'm taking Julia with me, you need to find yourself."

Dove stared at the television in the bedroom and remained silent. After they left Dove went to the kitchen to get something to eat, he looked in the refrigerator and found Lydia's forty ounce malt liquor. He sat in the basement, drank it and fell asleep. He woke up an hour later to his pager going off, he looked at the number and dialed it.

"Did anyone page Lawrence?"

"Hey it's me Roxanne, what's up, baby."

"Roxanne, Roxanne." Dove said UTFO style still buzzed from the forty ounce.

"What are you doing?" She said seductively.

"I'm chillin', my family left me for the evening so I've got time to myself."

"That's good, Why don't you come by the post office to pick me up. I need a ride home."

"Alright, I'll be right there." He hung the phone up, got into the car and drove to the post office. Roxanne sat on a bench in front of the Brentwood post office facility. Roxanne got in on the passenger side and Dove drove off.

"So how did you get my number?" He asked.

"I got it from Jake."

Once they arrived at her house she invited him in, they sat and drank Rum and Coke. Roxanne turned on the radio and played the WSOL hip hop mix. They were playing a hip-hop tribute to the Notorious B.I.G.

"I was a great rapper once," He said. "Then everything changed."

"Tell me about it baby." Roxanne sat so close to him on the couch Dove could smell her perfume.

"My partner in rhyme, my best friend doesn't need me anymore, I never thought he'd move on and rhyme without me. My wife doesn't understand, she thinks it's just a hobby but it's not. It's like my essence. I think God put me on this earth to rhyme and now that I don't it's like losing an old friend Youknowwhatl'msayin'?"

"I understand," Roxanne lied. "You two seem so different, how did you meet?"

"I met her eight years ago at the Lena Horne Film Festival, it was love at first sight. I knew she was the one, we're so alike and we're so different."

Roxanne used the stereo remote control to start the Isley Brother's greatest love songs CD. She took her work shoes off and placed them on his lap while drinking from her glass, while he rubbed her feet, she moaned. "Ooooh that feels so good."

Between the Sheets played. "This is my favorite song." She stood up and began slow grinding to the song.

"Dance with me." She pulled Dove off of the couch.

As they danced she wrapped her arms around him and they got into a slow grind. She looked Dove in the eyes, reached over and kissed him. He didn't fight it at first then he had a flashback to his first kiss with Victoria, he started to feel nervous. Then he had another flashback to the first time that he held Julia after ten hours of labor, he backed away from Roxanne's kiss and said. "I'm sorry Roxanne but my wife doesn't deserve to be disrespected this way and neither do you." He grabbed his jacket and got up to leave.

"But I need you, it can be our secret, I won't say nothing."

"But I will, I couldn't live with myself if I did this, but I can live with myself for leaving." As he walked out of the door Roxanne screamed. "You ain't shit, that's why your ass is so fucked up," She followed him out the door. "This is some good pussy you're walking away from."

"That's not what I heard." He laughed as he walked down the stairs to the car.

Dove drove home carefully and hoped that the police wouldn't stop him with liquor on his breath. When he got home, he changed his clothes, sat on the couch and watched *Wild Style*, his favorite hip-hop movie. Later that evening Victoria and Julia came home. Dove was asleep on the couch with the empty forty ounce bottle at his feet.

"Mommy, what's wrong with Daddy?"

"Only Daddy knows sweetheart." Victoria said putting a blanket over him. "Come on, it's time to take some medicine baby."

Dove woke up hours later and saw them both asleep in his bed, He thanked God that he didn't fuck up.

On Monday afternoon, Dove walked into Mood's building and passed his desk, Mood wasn't there. Dove turned around and saw him coming into the building with a bag from McDonalds. "I didn't know if you were still working here or not."

"Yeah I'm still here, I had to make a service run."

"What happened with that situation?"

"Mr. Blake stood up for me, he told Ms. Taylor that there were no complaints. He said that I was a big asset to the Royal Management Family and to this building. He's really very cool." Mood said smiling. "How are you doing?

Paradise told me you left while Hawk was rhyming."

"Yeah, I need to go talk to him, I was acting real stupid but I'm over that now." Dove said embarrassed.

"Now that sounds like the Dove I know and love."

Dove left to complete his route and drove over to the library, when Dove got there he saw Hawk talking to Rashad Morrison. Dove waited for Rashad to leave before approaching Hawk.

"Hey Hawk, you got a minute?"

Hawk looked at him expressionless. "Yeah, let's take a walk."

They walked out of the library and over to the hot dog stand in front of the abandoned Woodward and Lothrop Building.

Dove began. "Look I want to apologize for my behavior, I was jealous that you were rhymin' without me and because of the attention that you were getting." He paused. "To be honest I didn't think you could do it without me, when you got on stage I wanted you to be lousy but when I saw how good you were without me I couldn't take it. To make matters worse instead of talking about it like a man, I let it affect our friendship and my marriage. I've dealt with my demons, I was selfish and stupid and I'm sorry."

Hawk smiled. "Look you know how we roll, I'm glad you're finally talking about it man. You have a wonderful family and you've got to handle that, I promise I'm not going to be a star and leave you hanging. This solo thing is because I can't wait, I've got a hunger for this."

"I told Victoria the same thing."

Whenever you're ready we will be rocking stages together again, It always will be Hawk and Dove, you're like a brother to me."

"Thanks man." They hugged each other and started walking back towards the library.

"So by the way who won the contest?"

"Don't get me started man, the whole thing was a sham. Top Grade held the Insomnia Talent Show. All of their managers scout for talent to sign to the company and put them in a talent show, all are unsigned to the agency. Then at the last minute they bring in an already signed Top Grade artist who doesn't have to audition and who wins automatically. There were record labels there but only to check out the talent already signed to the agency."

"Damn, they brought in a ringer."

"Yeah we didn't even figure it out until after the show when all of us put two and two together. Rashad came with a contract that he wanted me to sign, I told him he could shove that contract up his ass. That's probably why Antigravity couldn't get into that exclusive audition, the thing that really pisses me off is he still has my EPMD tape."

Dove said. "Don't worry you can have mine, at least, you didn't sign anything."

"Word, that would've been a big mistake."

Dove's pager went off. "I need to find a phone real quick."

They walked back into the library and Dove called Victoria.

"Crestar, this is Victoria. How may I help you?"

"Hey honey."

"Thank you for the flowers and the poem, they are beautiful." Victoria said.

"I just wanted to apologize, with all that you do you don't deserve to be disrespected from the man who loves you."

"I love you too baby."

"You said I had to find myself, I realized I lost myself when I stopped rhyming and I took it out on everybody."

"I'll see you tonight baby so we can make up, maybe we can work something out."

He hung up the phone and said goodbye to Hawk, he jumped into his mail truck and drove away.

ANTIGRAVITY

"Yo! Where is he?" Flame said impatiently.

"I wish I knew." Raindance answered.

"I told you to tell him the meeting was an hour earlier, that's the only way to get him anywhere on time." Dynamite said not bothering to lift his head out of *The Source*. "I can't believe Biggie's gone man," Dynamite shook his head. "He's the only artist to make two covers of the *Source* back to back."

The members of Antigravity waited in front of Power Records for FOG, who was late again, they had a meeting with the vice president of Power Records Black Music Division.

"Yo, remember the time we had that show at the 9:30 club last November and FOG showed up right before we got on stage." Flame reminisced.

"Yeah." Raindance laughed.

"And he had all the beats on DAT." Dynamite laughed not taking his head out of the magazine.

Just then they heard FOG's stereo seconds before they saw his car round the corner. They saw his head bouncing up and down to Main Source's *Live at the BBQ*. It took him a few minutes to find a parking spot. As soon as he got to the building he said. "Sorry I'm late, I was cutting some hair and lost track of time."

They entered the building and got on the elevator, Raindance pressed the fifth floor button. The elevator opened into the offices of Power Records and they walked up to the lady at the front desk. "Hi, We have an appointment with Mr. Hobbs." Dynamite said.

The receptionist, who wore a headset, put her hand in the air and finished taking a message on the phone. When she was finished with the phone call she said. "Thank you for waiting, How may I help you?"

"We have a 2:00 p.m. meeting with Mr. Hobbs." FOG said.

"Will you take a seat? Who may I say is here?"

"You can tell him Antigravity is in the house." Flame announced.

She buzzed him on the intercom. "Mr. Hobbs, your two o'clock is here," She paused. "Yes sir." She took off her headset and said. "Will you please follow me?"

As they walked behind her, FOG, Dynamite and Raindance stared at her booty in her white hiphugger pants while Flame rolled her eyes and shook her head. She led them to a conference room. "Please take a seat, Mr. Hobbs should be here in a few minutes. Can I get you anything to drink?"

"I'll have a Sprite." Flame said.

"Yeah, me too." Dynamite chimed in.

"I'll have water." Raindance said.

She turned to FOG. "I'll have the same."

"Can we smoke in here?" Dynamite asked.

"No this is a smoke free building, my name is Synclaire and I'll be back with your drinks." Synclaire said and left the room.

"Did you see that ass?" FOG asked.

"She's the bomb." Dynamite said.

They looked around the room at the gold and platinum records hanging on the wall and at framed magazine covers of their artists on covers like *Vibe*, *The Source*, *Rolling Stone*, and *Spin*. A few minutes later, a tall black man dressed in a navy blue suit came in.

"Hello." He said as he smiled and sat down. "I'm Bret Hobbs and you are ...?" He asked while looking at FOG.

"I'm Andre Evans, a.k.a. FOG."

"I'm Miguel Garcia, they call me Dynamite."

"I'm Felicia Banks, a.k.a Flame."

"My name is Raymond Taylor or Raindance."

"It's really good to meet you," Bret said. "I don't

usually call in artists, we have other people who do that, but your demo was in my mailbox. How did you get my home address?"

"We don't have your address, we know your mail-man." Flame said.

"I see." Bret rose from his seat and walked over to the stereo, he popped the tape into the deck and returned to his seat. "I haven't listened to it yet."

Synclaire returned with the drinks. "Sit down Syn-claire, I want you to listen to this." Bret said.

Synclaire sat next to FOG as the music blared out of the speakers. The first song, *Melancholy Blues*, filled the room. The members of Antigravity looked at Bret Hobbs' expressionless face and watched him take notes after each song. The final song was a freestyle song over a basic drumbeat called *Off the Top*. The emcees freestyled the whole song. FOG turned to Dynamite, who shrugged his shoulders. Raindance glanced at Synclaire, who had her eyes closed and was feeling the music.

After they finished listening to the demo Bret asked. "Who's responsible for your production?"

"That would be me." FOG raised his hand.

"I see," He said. "So tell me about yourselves."

"We met about four years ago at a hip-hop talent show sponsored by WSOL." FOG said.

"Our styles complimented each other so we decided to form Antigravity, we're called Antigravity because our style can't be held down." Raindance said.

"We've performed all over D.C. including The Abstract Griot, the State of the Union and the 9:30 club." Dynamite said.

"I see," Said Bret expressionless. "Thank you for your time." Bret stood up. "Synclaire will show you out, have a good day." Bret walked out of the conference room.

The members of Antigravity just looked at each other.

"Yo! What just happened?" Flame asked.

"He's got a 2:45 conference call with California."

Synclaire said.

Dynamite turned to Synclaire. "Do you think he liked it?"

"It's hard to tell with Mr. Hobbs."

"What did you think of it?" FOG asked her.

"I loved it, especially the freestyle song. I found it refreshing."

"Thanks." Flame said as they rose to leave.

"I wish I could read his mind." Raindance said.

"Well he has your number, I'm sure he'll call you, Good luck and take care." Synclaire said showing them out.

They piled into FOG's car and drove downtown.

"So what do you think?" Dynamite asked. "Do you think he'll call us?"

"I hope so, that would be so cool." Flame said.

"Let's not lose perspective." FOG said. "We don't have a deal yet."

"FOG's right, We still have to practice for our performance at the Hip-Hop Reunion Seminar." Raindance said. "Let's meet at The Abstract Griot tonight."

"You're right," Flame said eyeing the Metro station. "FOG could you let me off here? I've got to get back to work."

"No problem." He pulled over.

"Peace, I'll meet y'all there tonight." Flame got out of the car and walked toward the Metro.

"Are we going back to the house or what?" FOG asked.

"Could you drop me off at The Abstract Griot?" Dynamite asked. "I need to look at my wall."

"Damn, Didn't you do that last night?" FOG asked.

"Yeah, but I'm still working on a concept."

FOG drove up to The Abstract Griot, let Dynamite off and asked. "Do you need anything from the house?"

"No I'm straight, I'll meet y'all here tonight." Dynamite said putting a cigarette in his mouth and lighting it.

That night at The Abstract Griot, Mood, Dana, Hawk and Paradise were in a booth playing spades when Flame walked in. She looked around the semi crowded Abstract Griot but didn't see anyone from Antigravity. She slid into the booth.

"Has anyone seen FOG, Raindance or Dynamite?"

"Not FOG or Raindance, but look out of the window." Paradise said.

Flame got up and looked out of the window by the stage and saw Dynamite looking at the wall intensely.

Jacob the waiter approached the table. "He's been out there like that for so long that people started giving him spare change."

"Damn." She looked at her watch, it was 7:30.

"He's been out there for hours." Hawk said as Flame sat back down.

"He's always like that when he's developing a concept for a piece." Flame said.

"I'm the same way when I'm writing a poem, hours on development but when I start writing I can be done with it in twenty minutes." Mood said.

FOG and Raindance walked in and took the empty table near the booth. "What's going on?"

"Nothing much FOG." Flame said.

"Anybody see Dynamite? When I dropped him off earlier he said he'd be here."

Everyone just pointed to the window Suddenly Dynamite burst through the door yelling. "I GOT IT!!!"

Everyone in the restaurant stopped what they were doing and turned toward Dynamite as he walked to his friends.

"I got it." He announced with his face beaming.

"Good for you, now what is it?" Dana asked.

"I can't tell you but I know you'll love it. I need to tell Kenny what I need, Has anyone seen him?"

"He's up in his office." Jacob said bringing some

cornbread to everyone at the table.

Dynamite ran upstairs taking two steps at a time to the second floor and knocked. Kenny opened the door while speaking into his cordless phone.

"Yes Dad I know, but that was years ago."

He told Dynamite to come in, Dynamite sat down in front of the desk and slouched in the chair. Kenny got off the phone and shook his head.

"That old man is gonna give me an ulcer, everytime I mention his band he complains about how they broke up. I don't know how I'm gonna get them on that stage without him ripping them apart. Are y'all still performing?"

"You know it."

"That's good, so what's up?" Kenny asked. "You finally decided to bring your ass inside."

"Yeah with some good news, I came up with a concept for the wall."

"What is it?" Kenny asked.

"No offense Kenny, I know this is your spot but I can't tell you just yet but it's gonna be the bomb." Dynamite said.

I can respect that, tell me what are you going to need?"

Dynamite slid the figures to him on a slip of paper, Kenny looked over the figures and pulled out his checkbook. Kenny handed Dynamite a check based on his figures and asked.

"Do you think you'll have it ready by the anniversary show?"

"Yeah I can guarantee it, I'll begin next Monday since we have to practice for the Hip-Hop Reunion Seminar this weekend."

"Wonderful," Kenny said. "Who's downstairs?"

If you're asking if Dana's downstairs the answer is yes but I think she's about to leave." Dynamite said. "I'd better go down and pay my respects." Kenny got up and left his office.

Down in the resturant, FOG was telling the story of their brief meeting with Power Records.

"No lie he was straight Stonehenge, no expression, no emotion nothing."

"Yeah," Flame said. "If he didn't like it, we sure couldn't tell."

"We should do a rap song about him." FOG began freestyling. "Like Easter Island, Hobbs wasn't smiling, not grinning, like the scarecrow in the Wiz singing, you can't win."

Everyone laughed.

Dana looked at the clock. "I got to run, I've got to prepare for tomorrow."

She rose to leave and hugged everyone. "I'm introducing my kids to poetry, I'd love for all of you to come to my class one day and do a poetry show."

"That's a good idea, let us know." Raindance said.

Dana got to the door and Kenny came downstairs. "Dana, you're leaving already?" He asked trying to look surprised.

"I can't start class tomorrow with red eyes and have my nosy kids talking about me, they already think I smoke weed."

They laughed and Kenny said. "It's good to see you smiling again."

"Thanks Kenny, it's good to have a reason to smile," She hugged him and said. "Goodnight."

"Take care." He watched her until she got into a cab and drove away.

Antigravity sat in a booth and planned their performance.

"Okay." Raindance said. "We got fifteen minutes on stage. That's enough to do three songs, we can start with *One Night Only*, do *Melancholy Blues*, and then get some subjects from the audience and freestyle those subjects. What do you think?"

FOG said. "I don't know, we always do *One Night*

99

Only, I'm getting tired of it."

"What if we do *Higher Plateau* instead?" Flame suggested.

"Yeah, I'm down with that." FOG said with a satisfied grin.

Dynamite said. "I'm going to the shirt man to pick up the Antigravity tee shirts tomorrow, we can sell the shirts and throw the stickers into the crowd from the stage."

"Cool," FOG said. "I'll get some more demos together so we can pass them out to record execs and the A and R guys."

"Word up." Flame said. "I'll be working all day tomorrow, so page me if you need me."

"Just come by the house when you get off work," Raindance said. "So we can work on the songs."

"I'll be there." Flame said, getting up to leave.

"Do you need a ride home?" FOG asked her.

"No thanks I'll take the Metro, I can pass the time by writing rhymes.

Flame walked up 7th Street to the Metro and took the escalator down, she reached into her pocket and pulled out her fare card. She hopped on the green line to L'Enfant Plaza where she waited to transfer to another train, she sat down, pulled out her pencil and pad and wrote some off the head rhymes when she heard someone call her name.

"Felicia, Felicia Banks."

She looked up and saw a woman with her hair in a French roll and dressed in a sequenced gown walking toward her. "I can't believe it, it *is* you."

"Oh wow! Lindsay Brown." She got up and hugged her old friend. "I haven't seen you since high school."

"I know it's been a long time, Felicia this is my husband Tom Vestor."

Tom was at least ten years older than Lindsay, she shook his hand. "It's nice to meet you."

"Very nice to meet you." He said in a deep voice, he was dressed in a tuxedo.

"Y'all look good, Where y'all headed to?"

"Well we just had dinner with Tom's business partner, he works for Anchor-Allen, one of the top law firms on the east coast." She bragged.

"Oh really? How did y'all meet?" Flame asked.

"At an art auction in Bethesda, we tried to outbid each other for some African masks. It was love at first sight and now the masks hang in our basement." She laughed.

Flame faked a laugh at her corny joke and asked. "How have you been?"

"Never better, the accounting firm that I'm working for is treating me well. Tom, in high school Felicia and I used to be like Salt 'N' Pepa. We used to wear our hair like them and everything."

Tom laughed.

"So Felicia, what are you doing now?" Lindsay asked.

"I'm working at the Tower Records by GWU and I'm still rhyming."

"Really." Lindsay said flatly.

Flame watched Lindsay's expression change.

"Yeah," Flame continued. "I rhyme with a group called Antigravity, we're making moves. We even had a meeting with Power Records today."

"Well... That's good." Lindsay said.

"Congratulations." Tom said.

Flame continued. "We're supposed to perform this weekend at the Hip-Hop Reunion Seminar at Howard University. Why don't y'all come and check us out."

"Well," Lindsay said. "We'd love to but we have plans this weekend, don't we honey?"

"We do?" Tom asked.

Lindsay flashed him a look. "Yes dear we do, I forgot about them."

Flame knew that she was lying. "Oh well that's too bad." Flame said.

When Tom and Lindsay's subway train arrived at the station the announcer said. "Blue Line train to Van Dorn."

"Well this is our train, are you going our way?" Lindsay asked.

"No, I'm going to Potomac Avenue."

"Well take care." Lindsay said as she jumped on the train.

"It was nice meeting you Felicia." Tom said as he followed his wife and boarded the train seconds before the door closed.

Flame watched their train pull off and shook her head. "Bourgeoise bitch, I need to get my degree."

Saturday the day of the Hip-Hop Reunion Seminar, FOG was getting dressed while Dynamite and Raindance waited downstairs in the townhouse that they shared. The phone rang, Dynamite picked it up.

"What's up?"

"Yo! Y'all ain't leave yet? What's goin' on?" Flame asked.

"We're waiting on you know who again."

"Damn! FOG's gonna be late for his own funeral, what time are y'all coming?"

FOG ran downstairs dressed in a pair of Black Timberlands, Army green khakis, a black t-shirt and a camouflage jacket. A black pick with a fist handle was sticking out of the middle of his Afro.

"We're about to leave now." said Dynamite, who was dressed in his red and white *Nautica* shirt, baggy blue jeans, beige Timberlands and New York Yankees baseball cap. "Make sure you wear a jacket, it's cold outside, we'll be there in twenty minutes. Peace."

Dynamite hung up the phone and reached for his red jacket.

"Has anybody seen my keys?" FOG yelled running out of the kitchen.

"Here," Raindance said. He was dressed in a pair of baggy denim overalls, a black turtleneck and a black knit dreadlock hat. He tossed the keys to FOG and grabbed his pea coat.

"Let's go, that seminar about independent labels starts in 45 minutes." He said.

They piled in FOG's car and drove to pick up Flame.

Raindance turned the radio to WSOL, which provided live coverage of the event. When they arrived at Flame's building on Pennsylvania Avenue, she was waiting outside. She wore a Chicago Bulls Starter jacket, a baggy pair of black jeans and a pair of Jordans. She flagged them down, Raindance jumped in the back and Flame sat in front.

"Yo! Turn that heat up."

"The heat's on full blast already Flame." FOG said.

"It's cold as shit out here, I can't believe it, It's the middle of April."

"Yeah I know." Dynamite said. "I hope it warms up by Monday so I can start on that wall."

When they arrived at Howard University, they walked towards the Blackburn Center, Paradise was there taking pictures and talking into her mini tape recorder. She wore a black and white wrap around her head, a black ankle-length skirt, her classic white Reeboks and a black coat. Paradise and Flame walked around to check out the people. FOG and Dynamite went to the second floor of the Blackburn Center, where many graffiti artists spray painted on big boards of Sheetrock. Raindance ran to the basement where the seminars were being held. He got to a door with a sign that read "Freedom: Starting your Independent Label." He walked in the door and looked for a seat, but the room was so full of people that he had to stand up in the back. He pulled out his notebook and took notes when he noticed Synclaire from Power Records, who sat in the front row with a pad and pen as well. "I wonder why she's here?" he thought to himself. Harris Bullock, owner of Boomerang Records, a company in North Carolina, gave the seminar. He walked around the room and made eye contact with everyone while he used a pointer on the chart. After the seminar was over and the room had cleared out Raindance waited for Synclaire.

"Hey Synclaire, What's up?"

She smiled. "How are you, …" She couldn't remember his name.

"It's Raindance." He said.

"Right from Antigravity."

"Yeah, that was a good class he gave." Raindance said as they walked upstairs.

"Yeah I know, he took next to nothing and made a success. You should read his book, *The Gateway to Success in the Music Business*. Are you interested in starting your own label?" She asked.

"No, I'm comparing the advantages and disadvantages of an independent label versus that of a major label. What about you?"

"I'm on a panel that starts in a few minutes called *Wanna Get Paid? How to Effectively Invest in Hip-Hop's Future*."

"If you're still here at 3:00, we're supposed to perform during the showcase in front of the arts building."

"I'll be there." She said while walking towards the room where the panel was being held.

"See you later." Raindance said.

Upstairs FOG and Dynamite watched an artist named Ozone construct a piece. Dynamite and Ozone met while they were students at the Corcoran School of Art. He now designs web sites for Designated Designs.

"So what's up Ozone?" Dynamite asked with a cigarette in his mouth.

"Nothing much man," He smiled. "It feels good to be out here without a tie on and to be able to express myself freely man, this is heaven on earth."

"True." Dynamite said.

"Your piece looks real good." FOG said with his hands in his pockets.

"Thanks man, but this ain't shit compared to that one

time when Me, Dynamite, Same and Fame bombed the wall of that Senator's house on Capitol Hill. He was the one who made those negative comments in the news about graffiti artists being vandals and gang members. Remember that?"

"I'll never forget that, that story even made it on CNN and we never got caught."

They laughed. "Hey man, are y'all ready to rock the house or what?" Ozone asked.

"Yeah, come on down and check us out."

A blunt that was going around made its way back to Ozone. He took a long pull, closed his eyes, and let the smoke exit from his nose.

"Man this is good, Y'all want a hit of this shit?"

"No thanks," Dynamite said. "I'm all right with this cigarette."

"I'm straight, it'll fuck up my breath control while I'm rhymin'." FOG said.

"Okay." Ozone said and passed the blunt behind him.

On the yard, Flame and Paradise walked past rows of vendors selling everything from fried fish to incense, perfumes and oils. They checked out the brothers and talked. "So I was writing rhymes and waiting for the Metro to go home and I ran into Lindsay, she was my girl back in high school, she loved hip-hop and wanted to rhyme as much as I did. Now she's married and an accountant, a career her father forced her into. She changed a lot Yo! When I told her I was still rhyming she looked at me like. 'Why don't you grow up?' You know that look."

"I know it well," Paradise said. "When I was working at Campbell-Jones I met this guy for lunch, on the way back to my office we stopped off at the Wiz so he could pick up that Sade album. When I picked up the Wyclef Jean CD, he looked at me and told me that hip-hop was immature and asked me when was I going to outgrow it. I told him I'll be rocking hip-hop until I'm well into my grave and I left his ass standing there."

Flame looked a little discouraged. "Running into her made me wonder if I wasting my time rhyming?"

"Well, what does your heart tell you? I've seen you on stage, I've seen that fire in your eyes. I've seen that little spiral notebook you write your rhymes in. This is your dream and you've got to pursue it, don't let what others thinks fuck up your destiny Felicia. She probably wished she had what it took, especially after those cats at Power Records sign y'all to that phat million-dollar deal."

"Yo! You are crazy girl." Flame laughed.

"Since I started to write again, it's the best thing in the world. I want you to feel the same and that will come in time."

They walked all the way to Founder's Library.

"Damn, we're missing the party." Flame said as they turned around and headed back towards the Blackburn Center.

When they got near the Blackburn Center Mood, Sabrina, Hawk, and Dana walked toward them. "Hey hey Damn it's cold, How long have you been out here?" Mood asked.

"We got here about 12:15, Paradise was here when we got here." Flame said.

"Yeah and I've been here since 11:30, I've been trying to get quick interviews with some of these rude ass emcees." Paradise rolled her eyes.

"We should have gotten here earlier, we had to park near The Abstract Griot and walk." Sabrina said.

"I met Dana coming out of the Metro and we met these two while they were parking." Hawk pointed to Mood and Sabrina.

"I'll be back, I have to go to the ladies' room." Dana said.

"I'll go with you Dana, I'll be right back honey." Sabrina kissed Mood on the cheek before leaving with Dana.

Flame and Paradise both said. "Honey!"

"Chill out with that." Mood smiled and blushed.

106

"Next thing you know he'll be carrying her purse." Hawk joked.

"Hardy har har," Mood laughed sarcastically. "Kenny said he'll be here to check y'all out at 3:00." Mood told Flame.

"Dove said he'd be here too," Hawk chimed in. "Right after work."

Dana and Sabrina walked back and were joined by Dynamite, FOG, and Raindance.

"What's up? The gang's all here." Dynamite hugged Hawk and Mood.

"The DJ competition is about to start." Paradise said looking at the list of events.

"Cool, let's check out that joint." FOG said.

While they waited in line Flame looked around and said. "Yo! That's Powerhouse, his album just went platinum, I'll be right back."

Flame approached him and said. "Yo, Powerhouse," She handed him a copy of their demo. "I dig your shit, now it's time for you to dig ours."

"I'll check your stuff out and pass it on."

"Excellent, If you're here at 3:00, check out our performance." Flame said. The line for the DJ competition started moving. "Yo! I gotta go." Flame ran to join her friends in line.

Inside the competition two DJ's were on either side of the stage. If you lost you were eliminated and the winner would advance to the next round. The winner of the competition would win $500 dollars and would be scheduled to perform as the in between act for the WSOL Hip-Hop Extravaganza at Constitution Hall in June. The competition was intense, DJ Pinto was doing some intricate scratching, but he got beat by Worldwide who played some old school instrumentals, including *Just Rhymin' with Biz* by Masta Ace and Queen Latifah's *Wrath of My Madness*. Worldwide had advanced to the finals and had to battle DJ Expression. Worldwide went on first. He transformed break beats with hands of lightning, while turning around and catching the record in time.

DJ Expression was next and started his set with *Buffalo Girls*. He started pop locking and scratching at the same time. Then he mixed a hook to a K-Solo song. "The lies, the rumors, the rumors, the lies" with the beginning of Salt 'N' Pepa's *Expression*. "The lies, the rumors, the rumors, the lies. It's all about expression." He went with this three times and suddenly the gym went pitch black. "Relax folks. Peep this." Expression said and scratched in Total's *Can't You See*. The crowd went wild and when the lights came back on, Worldwide knew that it was over and that DJ Expression had won.

After the competition, the group went outside and Sabrina shook her head. "I've never seen anything like that before."

"DJ Expression has won the competition three years in a row, he does a new trick every year and always tops himself." Paradise said.

"That in the dark shit was the off the hook." Hawk said.

Raindance checked his watch. "It's time for the showcase."

They walked across the yard to the stage outside of the arts building. All of the groups slated to perform were gathered outside. A group called Mad face, FOG's former group, was there.

"Well well well, look who we have here, It's FOG." The Shitstarter said.

"What's up man?"

"We're chillin', we ain't been doing nothin' but makin' moves since your punk ass left the group."

FOG sighed. "Why it gotta be like that?"

The Shitstarter got in his face. "You the fool who jetted, it's like that because you made it like that."

FOG remained calm and said. "Whatever, unlike you I

choose not to player hate Shitstarter.

"Fuck you and your crew, we got A and R from three different labels checking us out. Y'all ain't got shit, Y'all would be better off kicking that bitch out of your group." Shitstarter spat on the ground.

Flame jumped in the Shitstarter's face. "Who you callin' a bitch? I'll whip your sorry ass in a battle with my mouth taped shut."

"Sorry little girl," He waved her off. "But we're about to perform."

As the members of Mad face got on stage, The Shitstarter, Mayday and Uncle Fester performed their first song, *Mass Murder*, a grim tale about three serial killers and how each member killed their prey. The crowd loved them. Raindance took Flame and FOG for a walk. "The both of you need to calm down, he's trying to piss us off on purpose. We cannot bring that negative energy to the stage."

FOG calmed down. "You're right."

Flame remained silent. "I'm sorry Flame, he shouldn't have dissed you like that. That's just a tactic he uses to make people lose focus, he's just jealous." FOG said.

"Take that negative energy and refocus it." Raindance rubbed her shoulders from behind.

Flame closed her eyes and sighed. "Yo! I'm straight, but that's the last time I'm gonna be called a bitch."

When they returned to the stage, Mad face walked off the stage. A man approached The Shitstarter and handed him a business card. The second act was an emcee named Capricorn. He got on stage and rhymed two songs, *The Good Life* and *Five Hundred Channels*, a song about the brainwashing effect of television. After he finished rhyming, he walked off the stage to applause and into the arms of his wife and son. Antigravity took the stage and waited for the music to begin. The music erupted through the speakers and the members of Antigravity leaped into their first song, *Higher Plateau*. The crowd loved it. they bobbed their heads and sang the hook with the group, "Off to a higher plateau.

Rockin' microphones with my offbeat flow. If you see Antigravity, you came to see a show. Off I go to a higher plateau." The crowd roared in applause. Their next song was *Melancholy Blues*, a story about a saved girl named Melancholy who tries to save everyone around her, but no one listens to her.

After they completed their song Dynamite said. "What's up everybody? Antigravity's in the house. In the back we have the champion of the DJ competition, DJ Expression on the wheels of steel. We're gonna bust this freestyle real quick. We want to get some topics from the audience."

One guy yelled. "Rhyme about how it would feel if somebody killed your moms."

Raindance shook his head. "No, everybody rhymes about murder, give me something more complex."

A girl yelled out. "Rhyme about your favorite movie."

"Word, we can do that." FOG said. DJ Expression began scratching in the beat to Marley Marl's *The Symphony*.

DYNAMITE:
For obvious reasons, *Beat Street* is my favorite movie for all seasons.
Inspiring it gave me something to believe in
Back in the day when cats had heart
Like Spit and Ramone, I'd die for the art
Covering all four corners like the Roots in clones
Graffiti, breaking, DJing, and rocking microphones
Before record companies, we loved the local reaction
Starring Rae Dawn Chong who's now missing in action
Also starring Sequence
Funking me up at the House Party in the abandoned projects.

FOG:
Before NAS, Kurtis Blow rhymed about ruling the world
On stage pop-locking with a Jheri curl
Run screamed it was his house and we agreed

Wishing we was Russell when he was fuckin' Shelia E.
When Full Force left Russell limpin'
Featuring the Fat Boys, introduced by Donnie Simpson
My favorite movie of all time inspired me to rhyme
About the rise of DefJam and it showed and proved
The name of a RunDMC song called *Krush Groove.*

RAINDANCE:
When I'm live on stage, I like to bring the ruckus
The movie I loved the most was *Poetic Justice.*
It was good to see Janet in the hood with braids
Too bad she didn't stay
If I was Q-tip, Tupac, or the emcee that kissed Janet
I'd be hard like granite, respected around the planet
But could she really handle it? Or would she stalking me
Outside my house at 3:00 a.m. reading me poetry
Talking shit like little Penny when she was little Penny
Getting me tested to see if I'm HIV free
But would it be worth it? True, indeed,
Doing duets like Mary and Meth, you're all I need.

FLAME:
I get deeper and deeper like my name is Boss
My favorite movie featured Latifah in *Set it Off*
The only girl to face an Army with a handgun
About dreams that ended before they begun
Left Stony on the run for the South of the Border
Call the bank guy collect because she didn't have a quarter
Like Brandy and Tamia, I'll be missing you
Some guys think calling you a bitch ain't dissing you
But I'm here to make it official
Call me a bitch again and we'll see the bitch in you!

The crowd roared as she looked straight at The
Shitstarter. He couldn't say anything but his face was red
with anger. They left the stage to high fives and hugs and
walked back to the area where Mood, Sabrina, Dana, Hawk

and the newly arrived Kenny and Dove were.

"Damn, you left those mikes smoking," Paradise said. "I bet he won't call you a bitch anymore. FOG I can't believe you used to rhyme with them."

"Well they're still immature, My replacement Uncle Fester, can't fill these shoes." FOG kicked out his size eleven foot.

"What I can't believe is that Kenny is this far away from The Abstract Griot," Dynamite said. "I thought you were chained to the place." Everyone laughed.

Synclaire walked over to the group. "You guys gave a beautiful performance, you looked really professional on stage."

"Thanks," Raindance said. "Everyone meet Synclaire Moore, she works at Power Records."

They all introduced themselves. Kenny said. "I've been handing out fliers all day, I'm having a five dollar all you can eat buffet, let's go get some grub."

"Now that sounds like a plan." Mood said.

"Did Mr. Hobbs say anything about our meeting?" Flame asked Synclaire.

"No, but he usually has a staff meeting every Monday morning, we'll know something then."

They walked into the crowded Abstract Griot and enjoyed a good meal complete with entertainment from the Hibernation Crew.

Tuesday afternoon at Tower Records, Flame was behind the information counter. She looked out of the second floor window that overlooked George Washington University.

"Excuse me," A man holding a six month old little girl snapped Flame out of her daydream. "Do you have the new single *Janine* from Priest?"

"Follow me." Flame walked toward the CD singles. "Here it is." She handed him the CD. "Thanks a lot." And he walked to the cash register. As she walked past the CD's, she dreamed of someone asking for the Antigravity CD. She also dreamed about someday touring and performing in London and France.

"What's up Flame?" Paradise walked in wearing a black t-shirt, and denim overalls with a light jacket.

"Yo! Check this out." She lifted her left sleeve to show Paradise a fresh tattoo of a Phoenix rising from the fire with her name, Flame, in cursive lettering under the drawing.

"Wow I love it, Where did you get it done?"

"Dynamite works part-time at Fatty's, He hooked it up there."

"It looks really good, I was thinking about getting one too. Did it hurt?"

"It stung a little bit but it was worth it. I thought my moms would bug out when she saw it, but she said that I was an adult now and any decision that I make is my own."

"Well you are 23, so what's up?" Paradise asked.

"Well it's strange, Remember Synclaire from Power Records?"

"Isn't that's the girl from Saturday?"

"Yo! She called me up and asked me to come to Power Records, but told me not to tell the fellas about it."

"That is strange, What time is the meeting?"

"It's at 4:00, Can you come with me?"

"Sure but I have to cover a story at 6:00." Paradise said.

"Cool, I get off in a half hour." Flame said.

"Alright, I'll be downstairs looking at magazines until you're ready." Paradise headed downstairs.

At the end of her shift, Flame grabbed Paradise and left Tower Records. They walked to the Foggy Bottom/GWU Metro, and took the train to Farragut North. They arrived and went up to the office of Power Records. Synclaire was on the phone when they walked in, she got off the phone and greeted them. "Hello ladies, How are you?"

"Yo! Why am I here? And why just me?" Flame asked.

"I'll let Mr. Hobbs tell you that." She picked up the phone and paged Mr. Hobbs.

A few minutes later Mr. Hobbs came out. "Hello Flame, It's good to see you," He said. "Come to the conference room and bring your friend too." He turned to Synclaire. "Synclaire will you get us some beverages?"

In the conference room Mr. Hobbs said. "Have a seat ladies." He sat down at the head of the conference table, turned to Flame and said. "I asked you in because we're interested in signing you."

"Are you serious?" Flame said. "Wait until I tell the fellas."

"Congratulations Flame." Paradise said.

Then Flame asked him. "Why didn't you tell all of us together?" With an expressionless stare Mr. Hobbs looked at her and said. "We're not interested in the group, we want just you."

He presented her with a black folder with the Power Records logo emblazoned on the front. Flame opened it up and there it stared at her: a record contract. All of her dreams finally were going to come true, she flipped the pages very carefully and looked at the bottom page where she had to sign. Suddenly memories of Antigravity flooded her mind as vividly as scenes from a movie.

"Can I get an attorney to look this over?"

"Sure," He said. "Call Synclaire after your lawyer looks it over and we'll set up an appointment." He almost cracked a smile. He got up to leave and said. "I'll show you to the door."

Paradise remained silent until they got into the elevator.

"I can't believe it, you got a deal." She grabbed the plastic folder from Flame and looked at the contract. "I didn't know the process would be that simple."

"Yeah, but they only want to sign me," Flame said disappointed. "Not all of us."

"Wait a minute," Paradise looked up. "I know you're

114

not thinking of turning them down, this is what you worked hard for, this is what you quit school for. I will not let you throw this opportunity away."

"You make it sound so easy Paradise." Flame said as they walked out the building into the busy rush hour streets. "I'm part of a group, when we got together we became a family. Yo! I'd feel like I'm turning my back on them."

"If they're like family, I'm sure they'd want to see you happy. I know they'd understand."

"I guess." They got on the train and Flame got off at Metro Center. "Thanks for coming Paradise, I'll check you out later."

Flame got off and took the escalator up, and walked into the heart of Southeast D.C. She stood on the corner of Pennsylvania and Potomac Avenues and crossed the street and walked into the 24/7 store. She bought a pint of butter pecan ice cream and walked halfway up the block to her apartment building. Flame walked up the stairs and was overtaken by the stench of dry piss, she hurried until she reached the fourth floor and put her key in the door. When she opened the door, she was assaulted by the smell of fried chicken.

"Mama, I'm home."

Flame's mother poked her head out of the kitchen, the cordless phone covered her left ear. "Hold on Raymond, she just walked in the door. Yeah baby, you too." She smiled and handed the phone to Flame.

"What did you say to my moms?" She spoke into the phone.

"I just called her beautiful that's all." Raindance said.

"Chill with that, one Mood is enough. So what's up?"

"Nothing much, FOG's birthday is coming up on Monday and we're planning a surprise party for him at The Abstract Griot. Can you be there?"

"Of course, do I need to bring anything?"

"Kenny said he would handle everything, we just need to be there."

"I stopped by Tower, but Smiley told me I had just missed you and Paradise."

"Yeah we went to Pentagon City." Flame lied.

"Oh I'm glad I missed that shopping adventure, I'll talk to you later."

"Peace." She hung up the phone and walked towards her cluttered room. She laid on her bed and looked at the contract. Then she looked at the poster on the wall from Queen Latifah's "All Hail the Queen" days. "That could be me." She thought, but her thoughts quickly disappeared when her mother knocked on the door.

"Felicia it's time for dinner."

Later that evening at Harold's Barbershop, FOG was perfecting his famous shape up when Raindance walked in.

"What's up FOG? When will you be ready to go?" Raindance asked.

"This is the last head I'm cutting tonight. What's up?"

"I was thinking we could grab some grub at The Abstract Griot, Dynamite's still down there. When he called I told him to wait for us."

"Cool." FOG said finishing up his customer's haircut.

"Do you like it?" FOG swung him around to face the mirror on the wall.

The customer turned his head from left to right and inspected his head before nodding in approval.

"That will be ten dollars, you can pay at the register."

He paid and gave FOG a $2.00 tip.

"Thanks my brother, come back soon."

Then he turned to Harold, who sat by the register and looked at the latest issue of *Hustler*.

"That's twenty heads I cut and I've been here only four hours." FOG removed his smock and put on his green army jacket.

"Good work boy but tomorrow get here on time." Harold said not looking up from his magazine.

"Peace." They walked out of the door and hopped into

FOG's car.

FOG put in a Tony Touch mix tape that was full of new songs including *Stay Alive* by Wyclef Jean. "Where did you get this tape?" Raindance nodded his head back and forth.

"From that kid Rico, he's always in front of Metro Center, all his joints be bangin'."

At The Abstract Griot, Dynamite painted the whole wall with white paint. He had just finished when FOG blew the horn at him. FOG and Raindance sat at a circular table. Dynamite walked in right behind them, he took his paints and brushes upstairs to the second floor. He washed the brushes in the sink in the janitor's closet, sealed the paint cans and left them in the closet. He went downstairs and sat at the table. Mood came in a few minutes later and joined them at the table. Mood was still dressed in his suit.

"I just got back from the airport, Sabrina's on her way to Chicago to start working at that law firm."

"So how do you feel?" Raindance asked.

"I feel sad, I'm going to miss her. She said she'll be back in time for the Anniversary Celebration in June."

"You'll be able to see other people now." FOG said.

"We're gonna try to see how this long distance relationship will work."

"Are you sure you can do that? Chicago is a long way from D.C. Can you handle that type of commitment?" FOG asked.

"Well I'm gonna try, she's definitely worth it."

"Does her father approve of you dating his daughter?" Dynamite asked.

"At first he was rigid, but eventually he came around. You guys are like brothers to me. If I fuck up let me know."

"Well, I feel as long as you're not married or engaged, you shouldn't commit yourself like that. How do you know she won't be cheating on you?" FOG asked.

"I trust her, what we have really blossomed in the little time we had together, Momma Moody would be proud of her

117

baby boy."

"Well I'm proud of you," Raindance said. "FOG is talking all this shit now, he wasn't when Karen Spalding had his nose wide open."

"Yeah yeah but did you see her titties, I'd never stop breast feeding if I were her child."

They all laughed and Mood gave FOG a high five.

"Tomorrow I'm gonna start spray painting the wall." Dynamite said excitedly.

"What are you putting up?" Mood asked.

"Don't bother asking." FOG said.

"He's taking it to the grave with him."

"You'll love it, I swear." Dynamite told them.

"Have y'all heard anything from Power Records?" Mood asked. "They should have called by now."

"I'm gonna call tomorrow and find out what's up with them." Raindance said.

Kenny approached the table. "What's up fellas?"

"We thinking about calling Power Records to find out what's going on." FOG said.

"Well you should, you waited long enough." Kenny said.

"Yeah, I'm tired of waiting." Dynamite said.

They ordered and fifteen minutes later, the four of them ate.

After dinner, the three members of Antigravity drove home. They sat around the kitchen table and wrote rhymes to a track that FOG put together earlier that day in the basement. FOG decided to call Flame.

"Hello Mrs. Banks, I'm sorry to call so late. This is Andre, May I speak to Felicia?"

"Hold on Andre." Mrs. Banks said sleepily. A minute later Flame picked up the phone. "Hello."

"Hey Flame, we just finished writing rhymes to a beat I put together today. I'll bring you a copy of the beat tomorrow during freestyle night. The subject of this rhyme is Genesis, we all took a story from Genesis and rhymed about it. Do you have a Bible around?"

"How could you ask me that? I live with the most religious woman in the city." Flame sounded a little put off.

"Are you okay? You sound a little out of it."

"Umm yeah. I was drifting off to sleep before you called." She lied. "What time is it anyway?"

"It's 11:30, tell your mom I'm sorry for disturbing her."

"Alright, I'll see you tomorrow." She hung up the phone and sat back down on her bed. She picked up the record contract from her night stand and put it in her backpack, turned off the lights and went to sleep.

The next morning, Raindance went to his job as a telemarketer for Bell Atlantic. He spent the entire morning selling long distance packages and fighting sleep. He had stayed up until 1:30 in the morning with FOG and Dynamite, both of whom didn't have to be at work until late and could sleep longer if they wanted. At noon Raindance went to lunch. He went down to the cafeteria and used the payphone to call Power Records.

"Power Records, How may I direct your call?"

"Hello, may I speak to Bret Hobbs?" Raindance asked.

"He's out of town. Would you like to leave a message on his voicemail? He checks his messages."

"Is this Synclaire?" Raindance asked.

"Yes it is."

"It's Raindance from Antigravity. How are you?"

"Hey Raindance, what's going on?"

"Nothing much, I was just wondering if Mr. Hobbs expressed any interest in our group, It's almost been a week and…"

She cut him off mid sentence. "Didn't Flame tell you the news?"

"What news?" Raindance asked.

"I don't want to say, but maybe you should talk to her."

Synclaire said.

Raindance hung up the phone and called the house, FOG picked up the phone. "Hello."

"It's me, I just got off the phone with Synclaire at Power Records."

"Word, Did she tell you why they ain't been in touch?"

"I think Flame may have the answer to that question."

Later that evening, the Abstract Griot was full of people for freestyle night. Raindance, Dynamite, and FOG stood in front of The Abstract Griot.

"Like I said Synclaire was real vague about it, but I think they may have approached Flame with a solo record deal."

"But I don't understand," Dynamite paused and took a drag from his cigarette. "Why didn't she tell us?"

I don't know, but we're about to find out." Raindance pointed to the corner as Paradise walked across the street toward them.

"You think she knows something?" FOG asked.

"That's her girl, they talk about everything, I'd bet my skills on it."

"What's up brothers?" Paradise said as she approached them. "Why aren't you inside yet?"

"It's too hot in there, besides, we're waiting for Flame." Dynamite said.

"She's not here yet?" Paradise asked surprised. "She's never late for freestyle night."

"Maybe she's tied up at Power Records." FOG said.

"So Flame told you she got the deal?"

"No but you just did," Raindance smiled. "You may as well tell us the rest."

"I don't think so, y'all think y'all slick." Paradise shook her head and walked inside. "Triflin' asses."

After waiting outside for another fifteen minutes FOG said. "I don't think she's coming and the cipher is almost over."

They walked inside and joined the freestyle cipher.

The next afternoon Flame walked into the law office of Anchor-Allen and walked up to the receptionist's desk.

"Hello, I'm here to see Tom Vestor."

The male receptionist looked Flame up and down while undressing her with his eyes. Flame wore a black RIP B.I.G. and Tupac tee shirt, black wide-leg polyester pants and black boots. He smiled at her but never took his eyes off of her breasts.

"Ms. Felicia Banks." She said. "You pervert." She thought.

Tom came out in a blue suit.

"Hi Felicia," He shook her hand and said. "Come with me please."

In Tom's office, African art was everywhere and masks hung from the walls. He had a glass case with a collection of porcelain elephants and a painting of Cleopatra on the sands of Egypt.

"If you think there's a lot of art here, you should see the stuff Lindsay and I have at home." He laughed.

"Thank you for agreeing to see me on such short notice," Flame said. "It's just that I'm not hip to too many lawyers."

"No problem, any friend of Lindsay's is cool with me." He tried to sound hip. "So Power Records wants to sign you, that's very good. Do you have the contract?"

Flame reached into her backpack and pulled out the contract, she handed it to Tom and he reviewed it very carefully. He offered Flame some bottled water and some Godiva chocolate but she refused. He explained the contract to her, they spent hours reviewing it.

"Well Felicia, although record contracts are not my forte, everything seems to be in order," He handed it to her and took off his glasses. "Everything seems fair."

Flame got up, stretched and said. "Thank you for your time."

She began to leave. "Tell Lindsay I said hey and ask her to give me a call if she ever wants to hang out."

"I will definitely tell her," Tom handed her his business card. "Call me if you need further consultation or representation." He walked her to the door and said. "Goodbye."

As soon as she got near her apartment building, she saw FOG and Raindance sitting on the steps and waiting for her.

"It's about time you decided to come home Flame." Raindance said.

"Yo! What's goin' on with you?" Flame asked.

"When you didn't come to the cipher last night we decided to drop off that track to you." FOG said. "I think you'll like it, I sampled Queen Latifah on the hook."

"I'll work with it tonight." Flame said.

"Maybe you can use it for your first single." Raindance said.

"Alright who told you?" Flame asked.

"Well I called Synclaire Moore, after that we put two and two together. Why didn't you tell us?"

"Because I'm not taking the deal."

"Why not?" FOG asked.

"Because we're a group, it's all or nothing."

"That's bullshit!" Raindance said. "The reason you're not taking the deal is because you're afraid of change."

"You don't know what you are talking about!" Flame yelled.

"Flame, you're like a sister to me, I know you better than you think. You have never moved out of your mother's house, you've worked at Tower Records since you were eighteen years old and how many times have you said 'I have to get my degree.'? Life is all about change and opportunity, accept the change and take the opportunity. You may be the one emcee that will make people take D.C. hip-hop seriously, don't use us as an excuse."

Flame looked up at him and asked. "You want me to take the deal without y'all?"

"I would." Raindance said.

"Me too." FOG said.

"This is your dream, even if we're not by your side we got your back, don't cheat yourself."

The smell of fresh cornbread filled the air. They looked up to see Mrs. Banks staring out of the window at them. "Felicia, dinner's ready. Raymond, you and Andre are welcome." As they walked up the stairs Flame said. "I'm sure gonna miss Mom's cooking."

Monday night at 10:00, The Abstract Griot was dark when Dynamite and FOG rolled up. They parked and walked toward the door.

"Damn Dynamite, I can't believe you left your wallet, Why can't you just get it in the morning?"

"Man I told you I got money in my wallet, I don't want it gone."

FOG looked up. "It doesn't look like you're getting in." FOG looked at his watch. "It's only 10:00, I can't believe Kenny closed this early. It must've been a really slow night."

"I can't believe it either." Dynamite rang the doorbell to Kenny's office.

Kenny looked out of the window. "What's going on? I'm on a long-distance call."

"I need you to bring down my wallet, I left it in the janitor's closet."

"Hold on." After a few minutes, Kenny came to the door. "I don't see it, come up here and look."

They walked past Kenny into the dining area. FOG asked. "Why is it so dark?"

Suddenly the lights came on and everyone yelled. "SURPRISE!"

FOG almost had a heart attack. The place was full of his friends including Hawk, Dove, Mood, Raindance,

Paradise, Dana, Jacob, and Flame, who stood there holding a chocolate cake that was shaped like a microphone that had two candles. One was shaped like a two and the other like a five. The table behind Flame was full of gifts, DJ Expression was on the turntables playing old school songs from the year FOG was born. Kenny had a table with chicken wings, jambalaya, cornbread, and potato salad. A cooler was on the floor filled with iced tea, soda, and juices. Everyone ate and had a good time. Raindance got up and made a toast.

"Congratulations, you've reached an age not promised to many brothers."

Everyone at the table applauded. There was a knock on the front door, It was Synclaire. Dana opened the door and let her in.

"Looks like my party took a turn for the better, look who just walked in." FOG said.

"Hi everybody." Synclaire said.

"For my birthday, I know you got me a phat Power Records contract like Flame right?" FOG joked and everyone laughed.

She walked over to Flame.

"I called your house and your mom said you'd be here, Is there anyplace we can go, we need to talk."

"Yo Kenny! Can we use your office? We need to talk in private."

Kenny handed her the keys. "Lock it back when you're done and don't touch the papers on my desk, it may look messy but to me it's organized." He shoved a biscuit into his mouth.

They walked up to his office and closed the door to escape the noise and the music.

"What's up?" Flame asked.

"Have you talked to Mr. Hobbs yet?" Synclaire asked sitting on the couch.

"I'm supposed to meet with him tomorrow morning to finalize the deal." Flame sat on the edge of the desk.

"Don't give it to him." Synclaire said. "We had our

weekly staff meeting this morning. Mr. Hobbs just returned from our Los Angeles offices. He was talking to us about you. Once you're signed, he's planning to change your image and your style. He wants you to wear tight and revealing clothes and have you rhyme about sex and degrading yourself."

"He can't do that can he?" She said in shock.

"He can if you hand him that signed contract, I've seen people come and go. If Power Records doesn't want you to sell you won't sell."

"So its sell out or don't sell at all." Flame said crushed.

"I have an option," Synclaire said. "My dad just gave me some seed money and I'm using it to start my own record label. I've had this planned for the past two years, but had a problem finding the first act to represent the label, I want Antigravity to be that group. I majored in music business and have a minor in music theory. If you work with me, I'll guarantee that you will keep your publishing rights and we will split the profits right down the middle, half for the company and half for the artists. We will handle distribution and when you leave the company, you get full rights to your master recording. But I know you won't leave the company because it will be the bomb. My ex-boyfriend is putting together a movie soundtrack and I already secured a spot on the soundtrack for my artist. Are you interested?"

"I'm very interested, but I have to talk to the fellas first."

"I need to know something soon, they expect the song for that soundtrack in two weeks." Synclaire got up and left.

Flame locked up the office and joined the party.

The next morning Flame walked into the offices of Power Records at 10:00. Synclaire sat at the front desk.

"Tell Mr. Hobbs I'm here please."

Synclaire called Bret. "He's waiting for you in his office, Did you think about my offer?"

"Yeah, I'll be back to tell you as soon as I'm done."

Flame walked into the office. Bret sat in his office when Flame walked in. She noticed black and gold everywhere from Bret's Alpha Phi Alpha fraternity. "Hello Flame, How are you?"

"I'm good, How are you?"

"Wonderful." He flashed a rare smile.

"I talked to our A and R guys, we have great plans for you. Do you have the signed contract?"

"No I decided to decline on your offer."

"I don't understand what the problem is, when we last spoke you said you were ready to sign." He said.

"I changed my mind, I don't think you respect me as an artist." Flame looked directly into his eyes.

"I'm not sure I understand what you mean."

"I think you know exactly what I mean Mr. Hobbs, I'm not about to play myself for a record deal. Peace." She tossed the contract on his desk and walked out of his office without turning around.

As Flame walked down the corridor, she heard some noise in the conference room. She stopped and looked inside. The rap group Mad face and an A and R guy were laughing and drinking champagne. The Shitstarter saw Flame looking at him. He raised his glass to her and mouthed the word "Bitch." She shook her head and walked toward Synclaire's desk.

"What in the hell are they doing here?" Flame asked.

"Mr. Hobbs just signed them to a three album deal, he was going to put you with them and make you their "Boy Toy" female rapper. Did you sign?"

"I'm not signing with Power Records." Flame said with fire in her eyes.

"Well my offer still stands." Synclaire said.

"I haven't told the guys yet."

"Good, I'll meet you all at The Abstract Griot and we'll tell them together."

"That'll work." Flame walked out of Power Records thinking. "The more things change, the more they stay the same."

126

KENNETH BAKER

"Good morning, may I speak to Stanley "Mojo" Jackson please?" Kenny spoke into the telephone receiver while sitting at his desk.

"He's not in right now, you want to leave a message for him?" The soft female voice on the other end asked.

"Yes, my name is Kenneth Baker Jr. Mr. Jackson played in the same band as my father years ago. Could you have him call me? My phone number is 202-555-0103."

"I'll tell him you called." She said.

He hung up the phone and looked at his watch. 10:15. He looked at the huge desk calendar that had his list of things to do when there was a knock on his door.

"Come in." Kenny said.

Dynamite walked in. "Good morning Kenny, I was about to get started on the wall when I realized I need some more spray paint."

"How much money are you going to need?" Kenny reached into his pocket for some cash.

"About forty dollars." Dynamite eyed Kenny's roll of twenties.

"Just bring me back a receipt."

"No problemo. How's the quest of putting the band back together?"

"It's harder than I thought, Scat's the only member that stayed in the D.C. area. Everyone else is scattered across the country. I just called Mojo Jackson's house in Brooklyn and left a message, I hope he calls back."

"Well keep trying, It'll all work out."

Dynamite got up to leave. "I'll be back in a half hour."

Kenny picked up the list with the band's current phone numbers on it and dialed one of the numbers. "Hello, Mr. Lincoln Davis please."

"Speaking." Said the old gruff voice breathing hard on the phone.

"I'm glad I caught you, I've been trying to contact you for a couple of weeks."

"Yeah? Well if you're trying to sell me something I'm not interested."

"No sir. My name is Kenny Baker Jr, my father is Culture Baker, y'all played together in the late fifties and early sixties."

"Ha ha! Culture Baker, haven't seen him in a long time. How is that old bastard?"

"He's doing fine."

"Last I heard he had opened up a club in Washington. Now what was the name of that club again?" Lincoln's voice drifted off as he tried to remember.

"The Abstract Griot." Kenny said.

"Yeah that's it, How is that working out for him?"

"Actually that's the reason why I'm calling, I've been running for the club for the past five years. This June marks the thirty-fifth anniversary of The Abstract Griot. I wanted to surprise my father by reuniting all the members of Nomad for a performance. Do you think you'll be able to make it?"

"I'll tell you what son, If you could get me there it would be an honor."

"I'll have a train ticket sent to you, by the way, how's Philly?"

"Well it's a nice place to live. I'm back at school at Temple University. I have to complete only a few more courses to get my Master's."

"That's really good." Kenny said.

"Yeah, better late than never huh?" They both laughed.

"Thank you Mr. Davis, I'll be in touch Goodbye." Kenny hung up the phone.

There was a knock on the door. "Come in." Kenny said.

A woman walked in with shoulder length hair, she carried a big duffel bag.

"Hi, I ate here last night and left some keys on the table. Have you seen them?"

Kenny reached into his desk drawer and handed her a set of keys. "Here you go, I was hoping you'd show up." Kenny noticed the name on her duffel bag and said. "Fit Physique, are you about to work out?" He asked.

"I'm an aerobics instructor, without these keys I can't get into the gym, here's my card." She handed her business card to him. "Come by the gym if you're in the mood for an intense workout and ask for Lola," She smiled. "You know like in the song. 'Whatever Lola wants, Lola gets.'" She flirted.

Suddenly Kenny's phone rang.

"I better go, take care of yourself and give me a call." She said as she left.

"Damn." He thought as he answered the phone. "Abstract Griot, how may I help you?"

"Hey Kenny, it's me Mood."

"What's happening Mood?"

"Check this out, George is being transferred to the corporate office and is leaving to go to Chicago. They're having a party for him and they need the event to be catered. Can you do it?"

Kenny looked at his calendar and asked. "When is the event?"

"Friday at 2:00."

"That's workable, come by tonight, Cool Grooves will be performing. I'll have the menu ready."

"Thanks Kenny, I'll see you later."

Jacob came into Kenny's office. "Phil's here."

Without saying a word, Kenny followed Jacob downstairs through the kitchen and out of the back door where there was a delivery truck from Phil's Meat and Fish Market.

The driver of the truck said. "I have a delivery for Mr. Baker."

"That's me." Kenny said.

The driver unloaded the crates of beef, chicken and fish on his hand truck and wheeled it toward the freezer. After he was finished, he pulled out his clipboard and gave Kenny the invoice to look over. Kenny looked it over and made sure that everything was in order before he signed it. The driver gave him a copy and drove away.

Jacob looked over the inventory. "This order is more than usual, Are we adding more seafood to the menu Kenny?"

"It's a special menu for the anniversary show, I want it to be special so I'm adding more on the menu for that night."

Kenny walked back into his office and tried another number. A lady picked up the phone. "Hello, May I speak to Grover Bullock please?"

"Hold on please." She said. "Honey telephone."

He picked up the phone. "Hello, this is Grover."

After Kenny told him about the reunion Grover's answer was "Hell yeah! I'll be there, we had the type of band that could turn shit into sugar. Hey Ruth, Kenny's son is getting us all back together again to play at Kenny's club."

"That's wonderful dear, did you tell him we'll be there?"

"I sure did Ruth." He returned to the phone. "Listen I won't keep you, I know you're calling long distance just let me put this on my calendar. That's June 14th. Okay we'll be there son."

"That's wonderful," Kenny said. "Take care of yourself."

Kenny hung up the phone and looked at the clock. "12:30." He thought. "Everything was working out fine." Until the phone rang.

"Hello, The Abstract Griot."

"Hello Kenny, this is Pauline, manager of Cool Grooves."

"Hi Pauline, Is there anything you need for the band's performance tonight?"

Pauline paused and said. "No Kenny, I just got a call

130

from BET. They offered us an opportunity to perform as the backup band on Planet Groove, they're taping the show tonight. I know this is short notice but my band needs this type of exposure."

Kenny bit his tongue and hid his anger. "I guess business is business huh?"

"I'm glad you understand, maybe we can gig at your place in the near future."

"I never said I understood," Kenny said coldly before he hung up the phone. "Shit!" He said aloud.

He ran downstairs and outside where Dynamite was spray painting the wall. Dynamite sprayed figures on a light blue and white background while he listened to the new KRS-ONE album when Kenny approached him.

"Cool Grooves just canceled on me for tonight. Can Antigravity perform?"

"Raindance and FOG are in New York picking up some vinyl at a record convention," Raindance said. "They won't be back until tomorrow morning."

"Dammit, I need a group to perform tonight."

"Check this out," Dynamite lit a Newport. "Once a month there is a all female cipher that Flame, Paradise and Dana go to. One of the girls there rhymes in this all female rap band called Mahogany, I heard they're pretty good."

"How can I get in touch with them?"

"Call Flame at Tower, She'll know. Why did Cool Grooves cancel?"

"To perform on Planet Groove tonight."

"Damn, Those lucky bastards are gonna be close to fine ass Rachel."

Kenny went back upstairs and dialed Tower Records.

"Flame's on a break right now, Can I have her call you back?" The girl on the phone said while smacking her gum.

"Ask her to call Kenny at 202-555-0103."

"No problem." She said and hung up the phone.

The phone rang. Kenny picked it up, hoping it was Flame, but it was a man's voice that Kenny didn't recognize.

"Good afternoon, I'm Stanley Jackson. I'm returning the call of Mr. Kenny Baker, Jr."

"Hello Mr. Jackson, I'm Kenny. I called because The Abstract Griot's thirty- fifth anniversary show is coming up. I wanted to get Nomad back together as a surprise for my father. I was wondering if you'd be interested in coming to Washington D.C. to perform?"

Stanley cut Kenny off. "I don't think so," His response was cold. "There is no Nomad without the whole group and you can't bring Ricardo Lee back from the dead. The Abstract Griot used to be a good place to hear some good jazz, I heard since you took over the place has changed. All you young people with your damn rap music, I hate that stuff."

"What don't you like about rap music?" Kenny defensively asked him.

"It's not real music, It's stolen music. All you young people want to do is smoke marijuana and call our kings and queens niggers and bitches. You have no respect for life or your elders."

Kenny got upset but kept a level head. "With all due respect sir, what you said is not true. Not all rappers are disrespecting anyone. It sounds like you've been listening to too much C. Delores Tucker and not listening to enough of the music yourself."

"I don't want to listen to that bullshit. It's not doing anything but brainwashing our youth."

"I think you're wrong, our music is just as potent as yours. If you don't believe me, come on out here and listen to some of the rap groups we have performing. We are trying to reach out to you with our music, why don't you close the generation gap and reach back to us?"

Another call beeped in on Kenny's line. "Mr. Jackson, I have another call. Could you hold please?"

"Sure." Mojo Jackson said.

Kenny clicked over and said. "Abstract Griot."

"Yo! What's up? This is Flame."

"Flame, can you hold please?"

"Yeah."

Kenny clicked back to Mojo Jackson, but all he got was a dial tone. "Damn." He said and clicked back over to Flame. "Sorry about that Flame, I was on the phone trying to convince one of my father's band mates to come out, but he just left me hanging. I need a band for tonight."

"What happened to Cool Grooves?" Flame asked.

"They cancelled on me."

"I wanted to hear them too."

"Never mind them, Dynamite told me you freestyle with a sista who has an all female hip-hop band."

"You're talking about Calamity Jane, she has a rap group called Mahogany."

"Do you think they'll be available to perform tonight?"

"Here take her phone number and tell her that you're cool with me and Paradise."

Kenny wrote down the number and told Flame. "Come by tonight and I'll hook you up with your favorite meal."

"That's a bet, thanks man."

"Thank you Flame." Kenny hung up and dialed the number.

"Hello?" Said the voice on the other end of the phone.

"Hi, I'm looking for Jane."

"You got her, Who this?"

"My name is Kenny and I own a restaurant called The Abstract Griot. My show for tonight just cancelled on me. I heard you have a band and I was wondering if you'd be interested in filling in tonight."

"That's the place where Dana, Paradise and Flame have been telling me about."

"Yeah it's a good place to perform, Are you interested?"

"That shouldn't be a problem, the band should be here in an hour for rehearsal, we'll just marinate and be there tonight. What time should we be there?"

"Showtime is at 8:30."

"Cool, we'll be there at 7:00 to set up and do sound."

"You have no idea how much I appreciate it, I'll see you tonight." Kenny hung up the phone and stretched towards the ceiling.

At 4:00., Kenny had time to take a shower and change before he officially opened up at 6:00. He went upstairs to his loft, pulled off his sweat suit and started the shower water. He walked around in his boxer shorts looking for music to play during his shower. He settled on the Fugees: *The Score*. He selected his favorite song, *Cowboys*. Because of the steam coming from the shower, he could tell that the water was nice and hot just the way he liked it. He hopped out of his boxers and into the shower. After his shower, Kenny put on his black dress pants, a black dress shirt, and a pair of shoes. He passed a mirror and checked himself out. He wondered if Dana would stop by tonight, he walked downstairs. From the second floor, the smell of the fresh cornbread baking wafted from the kitchen. When he walked in the kitchen, Moms hummed Bob Marley's Wait in Vain while cutting okra and bell peppers for her jambalaya. Kenny walked behind her and said. "The cornbread smells good." He handed her an envelope with her paycheck in it.

"Thank you Kenny." She said and placed the check in her shirt where it rested on her bosoms.

"My my don't you look sharp, Is tonight the night you ask that sweet girl Dana out? She has a good job y'know and the two of you would make some pretty babies." Moms gushed.

"Whoa Moms, she's just a good friend."

"Good friend huh? That's what your mouth says, but not your heart."

"It's getting too hot in here." Kenny hurried out of the kitchen. "Kenny when you have time I need to discuss something with you."

"Yes ma'am."

Kenny walked into the dining area. He looked out of

134

the window and saw Dynamite talking to Dove. He walked around and entered the alley.

"What's going on Dove?" Kenny asked.

"Nothing much, I just left Howard's Sickle Cell Center." Dove shook his hand.

"How is Julia doing?"

"She's doing a lot better, She hasn't had an attack in a while."

"That's real good." Dynamite said.

"It's a blessing, I have to go now," Dove said. "Dynamite the mural looks good so far."

"Wait until I'm done, it's gonna be the bomb. People will come from miles and miles to marvel at such a site." Dynamite said as he stared at the wall in amazement.

"Don't let Moms hear you say that, She'll tell you they come from miles around for the food." Kenny said.

They all laughed and Dove walked over to his mail truck and left while Kenny went back inside to his office to get some work done.

At 7:00, there were a few customers eating when a tall lady walked in. She wore baggy jeans, an open long sleeve denim shirt and a baby tee shirt underneath. She wore her hair in plaits and had on sunglasses. She walked around and stood in front of the stage. Kenny walked up to her and said. "Hi, you can sit wherever you like."

"How about right there?" She pointed to the stage. "You must be Kenny, I'm Calamity Jane."

"It's good to meet you."

Calamity Jane looked around. "This is a real nice place you have here, It's got a pretty cool vibe."

"Thank you, I'm really anxious to hear your group. After you set up on stage, order anything you want for dinner. If you need anything just let me know." Kenny's pager went off. "Excuse me, I have to take this call."

"The rest of the group's outside, we'll start setting up." Calamity Jane said.

Within the hour The Abstract Griot was packed with customers, people ate and enjoyed themselves. Scat Strayer, Nomad's former drummer, walked in. Scat just returned from touring Europe. Kenny waited tables when he saw him walk in.

"Hey Scat, welcome back." Kenny walked over to him and shook his hand.

"Peace my brother, I'm glad I made it." Scat handed Kenny a present. It was the size of a framed poster and it was gift wrapped. "Look what I found in Paris."

Kenny opened it and it was an old concert poster of Nomad during their first European tour.

"I figured you could put this up the night of the anniversary."

"Thank you, I know exactly where I'm hanging this," He pointed at the bare wall behind the piano. "Right over there."

"That's a good place, How's your quest going to bring us back together?"

"Everyone agreed to it except for Mojo Jackson, he made it crystal clear that he wanted no parts of me or The Abstract Griot. He was real bitter."

"I'll talk to him, after his wife's death he stopped living, It's really sad."

"I'll let you handle it, I don't think he can be convinced."

Scat walked over toward the bar and waved as he passed the booth where Paradise, Dynamite, Hawk and Flame sat. They were involved in an intense game of Uno.

"What's up Scat?" Hawk said as Scat sat at his favorite stool at the end of the bar and ordered a drink.

Kenny walked over to the booth. "What's going on?"

"It's all good." Hawk said.

"Word up, I can't wait to see Mahogany perform." Dynamite drank his iced tea, slapped a card down on the table and yelled. "Uno!"

"Thanks Flame for hooking that up." Kenny said.

"You're welcome Kenny, Dynamite draw four." Flame slapped a card on the table.

"Oh man, it's on now." Dynamite said.

"What will you have?" Kenny asked.

"I'll just have the chef's salad please." Paradise said.

"Baked chicken and greens. Uno!" Hawk said.

"Ham with macaroni and cheese." Flame said.

"I'll have some of that jambalaya and some of that cornbread I smelled baking earlier." Dynamite said.

"Cool, It'll be ready shortly." Kenny went into the kitchen.

"Looks like I win again." Hawk said. "Y'all can't fade me in Uno."

Calamity Jane came over to the table. "Flame, Paradise, we're about to go on in twenty minutes. Paradise can you open us up with a poem?"

"Sure," Paradise said. "Jane meet Hawk and Dynamite."

"Twenty minutes is plenty of time for another game of Uno, you want us to deal you in?" Hawk asked Jane.

"I need more time than that to spank you in Uno." Jane said.

"Anytime you're ready." Hawk issued the challenge.

Mood walked in dressed in a navy blue suit, white shirt and striped tie. He looked around, spotted everyone and then sat next to Paradise.

"Mood, what's the word? You want to play some Uno?" Dynamite shook his hand.

"I can't stay, I just came by to pick up a catering menu from Kenny. Has anyone seen him?"

"He's in the kitchen, he's been helping Jacob wait tables." Paradise said.

Kenny came out of the kitchen and saw Mood. He walked over to the table and said. "I have to run upstairs and print out the menu from the computer, I'll be down in a minute." He ran up the stairs.

"Yo Paradise, Did Dana say anything to you about

bringing a date here?" Flame asked with her eyes glued to the door.

"She wouldn't do that, she knows how much Kenny likes her."

"Oh yeah? turn around." Dynamite looked up. Mood, Paradise and Hawk turned around as Dana walked in with a tall brown brother with a light beard blending into his close cropped haircut. He wore a black suit with a white shirt and black tie. Dana had her hair in a French braid and wore an evening gown. They sat down at a small table for two in front of the stage, Dana saw everyone and waved as they all just stared back.

"Maybe I can stay after all." Mood said.

"I can't believe she brought a guy in here, What's Kenny going to say?" Paradise whispered.

"I don't know but here he comes." Flame watched him walk down the stairs.

He walked past everyone and went straight into the kitchen.

"He didn't even see them." Hawk said.

Scat approached the table. "I know what all of you are thinking." He sat down next to Flame. "But this may be just the kick in the ass that man needs to ask that girl out. So just sit here and don't say anything to that man and watch what happens."

Having said that Scat got up and walked back to his stool at the end of the bar and ordered a drink.

Kenny came out of the kitchen with a tray of food and went to the table.

"Paradise, here's your salad. Hawk, baked chicken and greens. Flame, ham with macaroni and cheese. Dynamite, jambalaya and cornbread."

He placed the food on the table and gave Mood a manila envelope with the menu inside it. "If you need anything else, holler at me or Jacob."

Everyone at the table stared as Kenny walked over to

the table where Dana and her date sat. "Good evening, welcome to The Abstract Griot," He said to him and then turned to Dana. "You look really beautiful tonight."

"Thank you Kenny." Dana smiled.

The man said. "Excuse me waiter, but I'll have the Hoppin' John and cornbread."

"I'll have a baked potato Kenny. Kenny, This is Wendell James."

"Pleased to meet you." Kenny extended his hand for a shake.

"Likewise." Wendell said. He didn't look up as he lit a cigarette.

"Wendell, this is a non-smoking establishment."

"Excuse me waiter," His voice raised slightly "Don't tell me what to do, I'll report you to the owner."

"Sir, this is my restaurant and if you don't put out the cigarette you'll be facing a $300 dollar fine or can you read." Kenny pointed to the metal sign on the wall that read 'No smoking or be subject to a $300 fine.' Wendell put out the cigarette and Kenny took their order to the kitchen.

"Why did you want to come here to eat? We could have gone to the Occidental Grill or someplace more classy." Wendell said to an embarrassed Dana.

"I thought this was a compromise date, we eat where I want and we go where you want afterwards."

"You're right, I'm sorry but we must hurry." Wendell checked his watch.

At the booth Paradise said. "Did you see that? He tried to play Kenny."

"We should have all gotten up and..." Dynamite said.

"And what Dynamite?" Mood said. "Scat told us to chill and I'm gonna chill."

"We'll be back, we're going to the ladies' room." Paradise said, Flame got up also.

As they walked past Dana Flame pointed up to the bathroom so only Dana could see it.

"Excuse me, Wendell, but I have to go to the ladies'

room." She said and walked up the stairs behind Dana and Paradise. Wendell took the opportunity to make a call on his cell phone.

When they got to the ladies' room Flame and Paradise got on her.

"O.K. Who is he?" Paradise asked.

"Wendell is someone I work with."

"You're grown and we're not gonna tell you what to do, but why bring him here of all places?"

"We just stopped by to eat, we're on our way to the Shakespeare Theater to see Othello."

"Yo! What about Kenny?" Flame asked.

"We're just friends, If he wanted to be more than that I'm sure he would've told me. Do y'all expect me to sit around and let my coochie collect cobwebs forever? All we do is flirt while we're here and I go home to make love to my battery powered little friend."

"You got a dildo?" Flame asked surprised.

"I only pull it out during emergencies."

"So is Wendell the dildo's replacement?" Paradise asked.

"Or Kenny's?" Flame finished.

"It doesn't matter because I'm going to think of Kenny anyway," Dana turned to the mirror, checked her hair and said. "I always do."

"Coochie cobwebs?" Flame said and they all laughed. "That's funny!"

"Anyway," Dana continued. "We're out of here as soon as we've finished eating."

"We understand but beware of the stares," Paradise said. "I've got to go downstairs and open up for Mahogany." She said as she walked out of the ladies' room.

"Holler at us before you leave." Flame said as she walked out behind Paradise.

Dana checked herself in the mirror again and went downstairs, when she got down there her food was waiting for her.

"At least we didn't have to wait all day to eat here." Wendell said before he shoved a fork full of food into his mouth.

Dana looked up when the five women of Mahogany got on stage.

Calamity Jane caressed the microphone and said. "Hello, we're Mahogany." There was a light applause. "Before we begin we'd like to bring Paradise on stage to hit us off with some spoken word."

The crowd applauded when she got on stage. "Hello everyone, I want to dedicate this one to those sisters. I call this: *Thoughts of a Street Corner Mistress.*

Another hot summer night it feels about 82 degrees out
As I lean against a graffiti decorated wall.
My feet are killing me. Damn, I hate wearing pumps.
But in order to get paid and beat the competition
I must package the goods right.
I can see my reflection in the window
With my heavily made up face to hide the fact
That I'm only eighteen years old
Not exactly Daddy's little girl
Whoever he is, anyway.
All I have is a picture of him
Giving me a piggyback ride when I was three.
Never knew him and I don't want to know him
'Cause as tough as Mama is,
Her memories of him are the things that make her cry.
As much as I hate to do this I have to.
Mama's welfare ain't enough for her, myself, and my two children.
Yeah, I have a set of twins
Whose father turned out to be just like mine.
But that ain't nothing new fathers break out all the time.
I'm saving up my money
For my children to go to college

141

And to have the things Mama couldn't give me
While I was growing up
Because, without education they ain't going anywhere.
Damn, I have to go see Gina tomorrow
After what happened to her last Friday
Where a carload of college frat boys
Beat her down and took her money
And left her on the street. I thought she'd die for sure
But no one ever said this job would be glamorous.
I haven't caught any STD's and I thank God for that.
Here comes my first trick for tonight.
Check my purse for a condom. Good, I'm strapped.
Well, here goes.

Thank You.

Applause filled The Abstract Griot. As Paradise made her way off the stage, the five members of Mahogany played their first song, *Queen*. With India on the drums, Patty Wilcox on keyboard and Spice on upright bass, Calamity Jane and Pandora ripped vocals on the history of black women as Queens. The audience was impressed.

"Why don't they perform more around the city?" Hawk asked Flame.

"They're still trying to find their niche." Flame said bobbing her head to the music.

"Well I think they're pretty good." Hawk said.

"Yeah I know Now shut up, I'm trying to listen." Flame turned to Hawk and smiled, he returned her smile with a smile and a middle finger.

Mahogany's next song was called *Motive of Your Baby's Mother*, a song about deadbeat fathers. Halfway into the song Wendell and Dana got up to leave. Kenny watched them from behind the bar.

Scat looked and said. "That song must have struck a nerve." Dana waved goodbye to everyone at the table and left without turning back, Kenny walked upstairs to his office.

142

Scat went to the table and said. "That poor boy got a jones for that girl that won't quit."

"Obviously." Mood said.

"That's so sad," Paradise said. "What is he gonna do?"

"Probably throw himself into his work again," Scat said then he asked Mood. "What's this I hear about how some girl got you whipped?"

"I decided to chill with only one, she's in Chicago now."

"How is she doing?" Hawk asked.

"She's doing fine, she was supposed to come up this weekend but she said she's swamped with work and doubts if she can make it home, I was thinking about going to Chicago for Memorial Day weekend."

"Damn, I guess we're all getting old if you're settling down with one. Tell the truth though, she whipped it on you didn't she?" Scat laughed.

"Very funny." Mood joined in on the laughter, Hawk dealt a new game of Uno.

From his office Kenny watched Dana and Wendell get into his car and drive away. He pulled a glass and a bottle of Scotch from his desk, sat on the couch, poured himself a glass and drank it slowly. A few minutes later there was a knock on the door. "Come in."

Paradise walked in. "Kenny, Are you okay?"

"Yeah, I'm just taking a break. I'll be down in a few minutes."

Paradise sat on the couch beside him. "If it makes you feel better, she said he was just a friend."

He looked up at Paradise and said. "That's good, that's the same way she described our relationship."

"Have you ever tried to ask her out?"

"I'll never forget the first time I saw her, she was absolutely beautiful. That was back when I was bussing tables here and she went to Howard. Everyday she used to come here with this guy, I thought they were dating, later I

143

found out they were real good friends. One day I overheard him ask to take their relationship further, She said no and I never saw him again. A week later I asked her where her friend was and she said they weren't friends anymore because he took it someplace he shouldn't have. Later we became friends and I didn't want to lose her, so I never took it any further."

Paradise took his hand and said. "You need to follow your heart before it's too late to tell her."

"The timing has never been right," He paused. "He had the nerve to punk me in my own place."

"Don't let that bother you, I'll leave you alone to think."

"No, I'm right behind you." They walked downstairs.

Flame was on stage freestyling with Mahogany. Paradise sat down and Kenny made his rounds from table to table, thanking everyone for coming out, and making sure everyone was okay.

"Is he gonna be O.K.?" Hawk asked Paradise.

"I think so." She said as Kenny went into the kitchen, he came out with a pitcher of iced tea and filled glasses on the table.

At 11:00, The Abstract Griot was almost completely empty, Jacob placed the chairs on the table and Mahogany loaded their instruments into the van.

Outside by the van Scat and India were talking. "You have excellent technique and really good timing. How long have you been playing the drums?"

"Since I was six, I would go to school, do my home-work and practice on the drums for two hours everyday. My father was real strict, but my mother was worse. While my father worked on the weekends, I practiced for three hours."

"My band just got back from overseas and we're scheduled to perform here on Saturday. Why don't you come on down and check us out?"

"Most definitely." India smiled.

144

Inside Calamity Jane walked up to Kenny who was sweeping the floor.

"Thank you for letting us play here Kenny."

Kenny handed her an envelope full of cash. "Thank you for playing here, the crowd loved you. Can I schedule you again next week?"

"Most definitely, call me and we'll set something up." Calamity Jane said as she walked out the door.

Mood and Paradise were about to leave. "Why am I always the last one out of here?" Mood said.

"I don't know but the both of you get home safely."

Paradise hugged Kenny and said. "Stay peaceful."

"I will."

Kenny went into the kitchen where Moms put on her coat. "Walk me to the bus stop boy."

Kenny and Moms walked to the bus stop on Georgia Ave.

"Are you going to be okay? I can call you a cab."

"No, Franklin Junior should be waiting for me at my bus stop."

"How is he doing anyway?"

"He's doing good but he's havin' a hard time finding a job, you know, because of his criminal record and all."

"Maybe something will turn up."

"He's an excellent cook, maybe you can hire him to help me during the anniversary show."

"I already have four cooks, I don't know if I can afford another one right now Moms."

"He's willing to take whatever you can pay him, he was the head of a catering company in Lorton and catered events from the warden's retirement dinner to major weddings. He would ask you himself but you know how a black man's pride is."

"I'll give him a chance, tell him I'm looking for someone to head the catering service. Tell him to call and we'll set up an interview."

"Thank you baby."

The bus arrived, she kissed Kenny on the cheek. As she boarded the bus she said. "You're an angel, thank you."

Kenny walked to The Abstract Griot where Jacob locked up the front door. Jacob tossed the keys to Kenny and said. "I'll see you tomorrow."

"Take tomorrow off Jacob, you've worked two shifts today. I'll have Charlotte fill in for you."

"Thanks man, I could use the day. I'll take my family to the movies."

"Have a good time."

"I forgot to empty the trash in the kitchen." Jacob snapped his fingers.

"Don't worry, I'll get it."

"Good night and thank you."

Kenny walked into the kitchen and pulled the large plastic bag out of the trash can. In the trash was a crumpled up envelope with the Blues Alley emblem on it. He pulled it out and read it. Blues Alley was Moms offering twice as much as Kenny paid her. He wondered why she didn't mention it. Moms has been at The Abstract Griot for twenty years. I guess the discarded letter was her answer, he decided he wouldn't mention it if she didn't and knowing Moms she wouldn't.

Kenny closed and locked his office door and then went upstairs to his loft. He got undressed and went to bed in his underwear. He turned on the radio to WSOL's slow jam segment. The radio was playing *Adore* by Prince. Kenny immediately thought of Dana and sang the chorus of the song: "Until the end of time, I'll be there for you. You are my heart and mind, I truly adore you."

His phone rang, he reached over and picked it up. "Hello?"

It was his father on the other end. "Hey son, we just bought our tickets today for the show in June. We'll be arriving at National Airport on June 13th at 5p.m."

Kenny wrote down the information. "You got your

146

tickets one month early?"

"You know how your mama is, she don't do nothing last minute. How was your day son?"

"It was a little hectic but I handled it."

"I know you did, you're a Baker and you know our motto: We don't take no shit." He laughed. "When I die put that on my tombstone."

"Dad you know you're gonna live until you're a thousand years old."

"I know but don't tell your mother."

"Anything else Dad?"

"Your mother wants to talk to you, I love you Kenneth."

"I love you too Dad."

"Hi Kenny."

"Hi Mom."

"I just want to say goodnight."

"Goodnight Mom, I'll talk to you on Sunday."

"Okay baby, I love you."

"I love you too."

Kenny hung up the phone. He reached in his drawer and pulled out a picture that Paradise took of Dana and him during FOG's surprise party. He smiled as he thought about her and put the small-framed picture on his night stand. He started singing *Adore* by Prince, turned off the lights and went to sleep.

EPILOGUE

JUNE 1997

June 14th was the night of The Abstract Griot's thirty-fifth anniversary extravaganza. Kenny wore his black suit and his brand new black cowboy boots. He looked at himself in the mirror and began tying his tie. His father walked up behind him and adjusted his own tie. Culture was dressed in a dark brown suit, a white shirt, and a brown tie. He put on his beret that he began to wear since he started going bald and smiled at his son. "So son, you think you look good huh?"

Kenny rubbed his chin. "Dad I'm not trying to brag, but I'm the bomb."

Culture turned to his son. "You haven't seen the bomb until you've seen your mother, she just bought this dress that i guarantee will stop traffic, it even gave my old ass a hard on."

"Dad keep that to yourself." Kenny laughed and looked out of the window and saw Scat parking the rented minivan. In the minivan were the original members of Nomad who had survived. "Dad, I'll be right back I have to go to the kitchen and check on some things." Kenny said.

"Sure son, I'll see you when you get back." He looked in the mirror and checked himself out. "I'm a bad motherfucka ain't I?"

"Dad, you're one of a kind." Kenny laughed and went downstairs.

Kenny went to the kitchen and opened up the back door to let Lincoln Davis, Grover Bullock and his wife Ruth, Scat, Mojo Jackson and his daughter Eboni in.

"I need to sneak y'all into my office, follow me."

148

In the kitchen Moms and the other chefs were preparing dinner and baking cakes, homemade biscuits and cornbread. They followed Kenny upstairs to his office.

"I need to hide you up here until it's time for your performance."

"But we're scheduled to perform last, we'll miss everything." Lincoln looked around the office.

"No you won't." Kenny opened up the cabinet to his entertainment center, there was a huge forty inch color monitor. Kenny pulled the remote control out of his desk drawer. "This remote control operates all five cameras and those cameras cover the whole area. You can get a clear view of everything that goes on downstairs." Kenny turned to Mojo Jackson and said. "Thank you for coming, I'm glad you changed your mind."

"Scat came over to my house in Brooklyn and talked some sense into me, I'm sorry I treated you like a child."

"Apology accepted." He shook Mojo's hand. "Eboni, you can come downstairs, my father doesn't know you, but he may recognize you Mrs. Bullock. You may have to watch from up here as well. Maybe you can come down when it gets crowded."

"Don't worry about me sugar." Mrs. Bullock sat on the couch and relaxed.

"I'll make sure Jacob takes care of everything you need including dinner and drinks, when the time is right Scat will come and get you."

Eboni, Scat and Kenny left the office and walked downstairs.

"I have to run home and get ready." Scat said. "I'll be back here in about an hour." He went through the kitchen and out of the back door where the minivan was parked and then drove home.

"Is it hard running a restaurant?" Eboni asked.

"It has its moments, but I love my job. What do you do?"

"I work at Con Edison, I'm an executive secretary."

"Is this your first time in D.C.?"

"I haven't been here since I was ten, I came here with my class to see the White House."

"How old are you now?"

"I'm 27."

They sat at one of the tables and she said. "Thank you for this. Since my father came here and hooked up with his friends he's smiling again, he hasn't been this happy since my mom was still alive."

"Well I'm glad I was able to help, I know it's hard to go on after losing people you love."

The place was still empty but beautifully decorated. There were more tables filling the floor than usual and they were topped with all red tablecloths. On each table, there was a program that contained a schedule of performances, the history of The Abstract Griot and a special menu that included crabs, potato-crusted salmon, shrimp, lobster and steak.

"I'll be right back Eboni, I have to check on my parents.

"I'll see you in a little while." Eboni pulled a Jet magazine out of her purse.

Upstairs Culture was reading the Weekend section of the *Washington Post*. There was an article about tonight's anniversary dinner and show. There was a picture of Kenny in the front of the place and pointing at the sign that said. "Welcome to The Abstract Griot established in 1962."

"This is a good picture, I wonder what's taking your mother so long." Culture stared at his watch.

Polly was still in the bathroom getting ready. Culture saw his upright bass in the corner and said. "I can't believe you kept that old thing."

"Well throwing it away would be like throwing away my heritage."

"I'm glad I raised a compassionate and sensible black man." Culture patted Kenny on the back.

"Sensible?"

"Yeah, you had sense enough to avoid an ass-whippin'. I would have to cut ya if anything happened to my bass." He smiled and they both laughed.

Polly came out of the bathroom wearing a short pink dress that showed off her legs. "I can't believe how good this old storage room looks. Honey, we should've turned this into an apartment, think of all that rent money we could've saved."

"The reason I did it was because I got tired of turning the office couch into my bed. There have been some nights I'd work until it was morning. Then I would have to travel clear across town to shower, change and come back here. This saves time and money," He looked at his mother and said "You look lovely tonight."

"Thank you Kenny," She turned to Culture. "That should've been the first thing out of your mouth."

"I couldn't talk because your beauty left me breathless." Culture turned to his son and winked his eye.

"Ready to go downstairs?" Kenny asked.

"Let's go." Culture extended his arm out so his wife could take it.

Later that evening, the anniversary show was in full swing as the jazz quartet Soul Call set the place on fire with a stunning rendition of the War classic, *The World Is a Ghetto*. Hawk looked cool in his dark green polo shirt, baggy black jeans and black Kangol. He sat in a booth with Paradise, who wore a tan mini dress and a pair of heeled slides that exposed her airbrushed toes. Her locks had grown and were sticking straight up in the air. Dana walked in dressed in a sky blue sun dress, a pair of sandals.

She slid in the booth next to Hawk. "Hi." Her wide smile exposed all her teeth.

"Hey Dana," Hawk said freaked out by her smile. "My what big teeth you have."

"Hi," Paradise noticed the smile. "What's going on with you?"

"Everything is great, I was a little depressed after my

151

class graduated yesterday. I'm gonna miss them, they looked so good in their caps and gowns."

Dana pulled pictures from her purse and passed them around the table.

"I was contemplating what I was going to do this summer, I didn't know if I was going to travel or teach. I got this letter in the mail today, It's from Lisa, the student that was assaulted." Dana pulled out the letter and read it:

"Dear Ms. Coleman

Thank you for being the first teacher to care. I'll never forget what happened to me and I'll never forget you. Georgia is really nice, my grandmother has a big backyard, I have a puppy and a lot of new friends. My family was real poor and we couldn't afford a lawyer to fight Mr. Stevens. But my mother said if I keep praying to God, I'll get over my experience with Mr. Stevens. I hope she's right. Take care of yourself and write me back.

God bless you.
Lisa

P.S. Now I know what I want to be when I grow up."

"I cried after I read it, I actually inspired someone. I decided to let this letter inspire me, I'm going to volunteer my time this summer at a workshop helping children cope with abuse."

"That's beautiful," Hawk said. "Come by the library on Monday, I'll help you get some information together and a list of places that can benefit from your help."

"Thank you Hawk," Dana said. "But the cherry on the

152

top of the sundae was this article that was on the front page of the Metro section of the *Washington Post.*"

She pulled out a folded copy of the Metro section. The headline read. "Suburban Teacher Convicted Faces Maximum Sentence in the Rape of Policeman's Daughter." There was a picture of Mr. Stevens under the headline.

"By the time they're done with him he'll be under the jail, I guess prayer works after all."

"Amen to that." Paradise said.

Flame walked in dressed in a pair of baggy jeans, a new pair of white Nikes Air Force Ones and a blue sweater vest with no shirt underneath. She was followed by Mood, who wore a pair of beige linen pants, a white Nautica button down short sleeve shirt and a pair of leather sandals. They both sat down in the booth.

"Flame, where's your crew?" Paradise asked. "Aren't y'all scheduled to go on soon?"

"They're on the way, FOG had trouble starting his car. I called Mood and he picked me up."

"Is Sabrina still coming?" Dana asked.

"Yeah her friend Melanie picked her up from the airport last night." He looked at his watch. "She said she had something important to tell me, and I've given it a lot of thought. Tonight's the night I'm going to tell her that I love her."

"Don't do it man." Hawk joked.

"I've never felt like this for a woman before." Mood blushed.

"You've definitely come a long way." Paradise said.

"For real, you were a straight up dog." Flame said.

"I'm proud of you Mood," Dana patted him on the back. "Isn't love a beautiful feeling?"

"It sure is, I can't wait to see her, I miss her so much."

"Awwww." Everyone at the table said in unison.

"You know that once you say those three words, you have to give up your playa's card." Hawk said.

"It don't even matter." Mood smiled.

153

Kenny walked out of the kitchen and toward the table. "Hey gang, what's going on?"

"Hi Kenny," Dana said. "The place looks nice."

"We're really proud of you." Mood reached out to shake his hand.

"Thank you, I want to thank all of you for agreeing to perform. See that girl over there?" Kenny pointed to Eboni in the corner. "That's Mojo Jackson's daughter, her father is in my office waiting for their surprise performance. Can she sit here with you so she won't be lonely?"

"Sure." Mood said.

"Yeah Kenny, bring her over." Hawk said.

"Thanks." Kenny called her over to the table.

Hawk looked and said. "Damn she's cute! Mood, I might be turning in my playa's card too."

Everyone at the table laughed.

"Eboni, I'd like you to meet my friends: Mood, Hawk, Paradise, Dana, and Flame."

"It's nice to meet you all." She said shyly.

"We saw you sitting there alone, Why don't you join us?" Dana asked.

"Thank you."

Flame moved over and made room for her to sit down.

"I've got to get back to work, call me if you need anything." Kenny walked by his mother and father's table.

"C' mere boy." Culture called him over to the table.

Soul Call played their final song, *Island Dreams*. Raindance, Dynamite and FOG walked in and grabbed the empty table next to the booth. They all wore the new Antigravity tee shirts that Dynamite had designed. Raindance wore baggy jeans. FOG had on a pair of Guess shorts, and Dynamite wore a pair of sweat pants. Dynamite handed Flame a medium tee shirt.

"What time do we go on?" Dynamite asked Flame.

"We're supposed to go on after Paradise." Flame said.

"And I'm about to go on next." Paradise dug in her backpack for her book of poetry.

"Fellas, this is Eboni. Eboni, these are my partners FOG, Dynamite, and Raindance." Flame introduced them.

Eboni looked at the tee shirt and put two and two together. "Are you the same Antigravity with the song on the radio named *Elements of a Battle*?

"That's us." FOG said proudly.

"You guys are blowing up, I thought you were from New York."

"Thank you," Raindance said. "We appreciate the love."

"I bought the whole *Poetic Suite* soundtrack, yours and Maxwell's song are the only two that I like." Eboni gushed.

"Fellas, I think we have a fan." Dynamite said.

"You have a table full of fans," Dana said. "Now are you going to tell us what you spray painted on the wall under the tarp?"

"You'll find out in a few hours." Dynamite said relishing the anticipation.

Dove walked in dressed in a black suit, a royal blue shirt, and a yellow and blue tie. By his side was his wife Victoria, who wore a gold mini dress and a pair of high heeled shoes. Hawk got up and gave his friends a hug.

"Thanks for coming out but you didn't have to get all dressed up."

"We're going on a midnight cruise aboard the Spirit of Washington after we leave here." Dove turned to Victoria. "Come on honey, I want you to meet my friends."

After he introduced everyone to Victoria they sat down at a table for two and ordered dinner.

Kenny took the stage. "That was Soul Call, next up we have someone who's been coming here for three years. She used to be too shy to read on poetry night, Now the world's her stage. She's a staff writer for the *D.C. City Reader* and a contributor to the *Washington Post*. I present Ms. Evelyn Patterson better known as Paradise."

The auidience clapped.

"Thank you," Paradise said. "The piece that I'm about to share with you is important to me, It's called

155

MY CROWNING GLORY

Every lock and twist represents
A great one that I miss
From Sojourner to Ella to Betty Shabazz
My crowning glory represents blackness like jazz.

My crowning glory is a legacy
Something you don't understand and cannot see
You've called me Buckwheat, Farina, both a disgrace
And your disrespect of my sisterhood is not advancing our
race.

In its place, you want fried, dyed, and laid to the side
But my crowning glory is free from slavery
To fulfill its own destiny
It can no longer be denied.

Rest all your preconceived stereotypes
Worn by kings, queens, as well as Christ.
My crowning glory is an optical poem
Telling a story in its own natural form.

A story as mysterious as the Pyramids
My crowning glory houses treasures
Like a field of dreams.
My crowning glory is vast and beautiful.

Like the waves crashing to the shore,
My crowning glory tells a story
Like the Garden of Eden.
My crowning glory is Paradise.

Thank you."

    Paradise received a standing ovation.
    "Thank you." Was all that she could muster.

Inside she was so overjoyed that this, her most personal poem, was so well received. Her eyes started welling up with tears and she couldn't even do the other two poems that she planned on reciting. She left the stage and returned to her table.

"Yo! When did you write that poem?" Flame asked.

"The night I quit my job at Campbell-Jones."

"Why haven't you read it before?" Flame asked.

"It was really personal, I wrote it to give it some closure."

"That was a really beautiful poem, It was really deep." Eboni said.

"Thank you, I'm glad you enjoyed it." Paradise sat down and wiped her eyes with a napkin.

Mood wondered why Sabrina was so late, he decided to call her house. He went upstairs to the payphones and called her house.

Mr. Blake picked up the phone. "Hello?"

"Hello Mr. Blake, this is Theodore. I was calling to see if Sabrina was still there or if she left to meet me."

"Theodore, Sabrina's not here, she's in Chicago."

"Are you sure? I called her yesterday and she said she'd be here for The Abstract Griot's anniversary show."

"Well, I just talked to her ten minutes ago and she was at home getting ready to go out with George."

Mood was devastated but tried his best to hide it. "Oh I see, I must have misunderstood her. I'm sorry to bother you, have a good night."

"I'll see you on Monday." Mr. Blake said flatly.

Mood walked downstairs. He sat at the table and didn't say anything.

"What's wrong?" Dana asked.

"Nothing." Mood said embarrassed.

Synclaire walked in wearing a pair of tight blue jeans and a white shirt with a small button that read "Sparkle Entertainment." Named after the nickname that her father gave to her.

157

"You're just in time, we're about to go on next." FOG said.

She sat at the table with FOG, Dynamite and Raindance. Flame left the booth and joined them at the table.

Synclaire began, "When I was working at Power Records I made a lot of contacts, but leaving Power Records was the best thing I could've done. Bret Hobbs laughed under his breath as he wished me luck with my one act and my dreams. Your song was the first to be released from the *Poetic Suite* soundtrack and is blowing up all over the east coast. I just got a call from the people involved with the Smokin' Groove tour. Pack your bags! This summer, we're going to be the opening act for the Smokin' Grooves '97 with George Clinton, Cypress Hill, Erykah Badu, The Roots and Foxy Brown!"

They screamed so loud that everyone in the place stared at them.

"We leave for the Smokin' Grooves' Tour in one month and next week we will shoot our video for *Elements of a Battle*."

"Where are we going to shoot the video?" Flame asked.

"I have to be honest, we won't have a lot of money to shoot anything major. Just a performance video to introduce the group."

"Let's do it here." Raindance said.

"That's a good idea." FOG said.

"I'll come by your place tomorrow and we'll discuss some ideas for the video." Synclaire said. "Right now why don't you get on stage and rock the house."

Mood looked up as Melanie, Sabrina's friend walked in. She looked around until she spotted Mood and walked over to him.

"Mood, Sabrina is not going to be able to make it tonight, she has a function with her parents that came up at the last minute. When she came on such short notice her parents assumed she was there for the function and won't let her come out tonight."

"You can save it, I called her house and talked to her father. I also know about her and George." Mood said. "And she had the nerve to send you to cover up for her. How long have they been going out?"

"The first week that he arrived in Chicago, at first her father pressured her to go out with him and show him around Chicago. Then they started seeing more of each other because the only way to see Chicago is at night with all the jazz and blues clubs they have."

"I guess that's why she didn't want me to come up for Memorial Day weekend, she claimed she had too much work and wouldn't have time to hang out." Mood figured.

"George getting that promotion and raise helped too, she's my girl and all but she was raised with money. When she was weighing you and George on a scale, the fact that he's close, has money and has a good relationship with her father weighed more than a long-distance relationship with a broke poet who gets her father's shirts dry cleaned." Melanie said without apology.

"When was she going to tell me?" Mood asked.

"She probably wasn't, she would've kept stringing you until you initiated the breakup so she wouldn't feel so guilty."

"Damn." Mood shook his head. "Thanks for being so honest Melanie."

She patted him on the back. "If it's any consolation, I told her she was a fool."

"Thanks, Did you pass the bar?"

"On my first try, I'm going to start my own entertainment law firm. Why devote all my time and energy making someone else richer?"

"In that case, there is someone I'd like you to meet." Mood brought her over to Antigravity's table to meet Synclaire. "Synclaire, I'd like you to meet Melanie. Melanie is practicing entertainment law. Synclaire has just started her label and this is her first act, Antigravity."

"I hear your song on the radio all the time, you cats are blowing up the spot."

"Thanks." Raindance said.

"Here's my number." Melanie said. "Call me if you need a lawyer."

"I'll definitely give you a call, maybe we can meet Monday to discuss some contracts." Synclaire said.

"That's great." Melanie said.

Kenny walked up to the stage and said. "Ladies and gentlemen, are you enjoying the evening?"

There was a round of applause in response to his question.

"Next up to perform is a group whose song, *Elements of a Battle*, been blowing up on WSOL and is about to take America by storm. Give it up for Antigravity!!! The room filled with applause as Raindance, FOG, Flame and Dynamite climbed up to the stage. DJ Expression cut in the instrumental to their song, *African Traditions* and Antigravity began to rhyme.

FOG:
I regulate like Warren G
Peace to my bros, my foes have to pay a fee
It's me FOG fucking up your 20/20s
Rhyme against me you'll be singled out like Jenny
The train is coming so people get ready
Don't worry if you're late we're making Infinite Loops like Heady
Breakin' in a B-boy stance like Rock Steady
I'd rhyme all day if you'd let me
Don't ever deny the fact I've got the gift
And I Bust more rhymes than Trevor Smith

FLAME:
Almost counts only in Horseshoes and hand grenades
Before you battle me bring your whole brigade

160

Don't come alone
I'll leave you lost in the Atlantic like Sylvia Rhone
I come with more essence than Susan Taylor's presence
You need to leave on the same boat you came on
Want to hear me rhyme all you got to say is 'Flame on'
And like Johnny Storm, lyrically I burn
And when I corner that ass, where will you turn?
You'll be Krusty like the clown, a crispy recipe like KFC
I'll turn your ass from a sergeant to a PFC
Hope to be dope as me
Better join the Army to be all you can be
That's the closest you'll get to 100 percent
While I get more cheers than Ted Danson or George Wendt

DYNAMITE:
Rough as TNT, I'll blow you out the park
You want to battle me, but you don't have the heart
In the back of the crowd, you sit back mad stressed
I'll have you screaming dynamite like JJ in the projects
The object of my affection
Is this microphone that's under my protection
I'm Puerto Rican, not Mexican, so I say Que' Pasa
Like Kid Frost, I'm representing for La Raza
Bet against me, I guarantee ya lost dollars
Like heads investing in Cross Colours

RAINDANCE:
I tear down walls like Berlin
Cast spells like Merlin
You're local, I've traveled around the world that's turning
I gets down for mine, Word is born
Raindance around a Flame to create a Quiet Storm
On a plane so high like Doug E. Fresh
With the Get Fresh Crew after Slick Rick left
Every breath you take like the Police you're being watched
Like you're on the People's Court with Judge Ed Koch
I bring more love than Joanie and Chachi

But I'm still a desperado like El Mariachi
Fuck Ghostbusters, I'm the one to call
Now you're Buggin' Out like a spot with no black folks on
the wall

After their freestyle, they performed *Higher Plateau* and *Melancholy Blues* before they did their current single, *Elements of a Battle*. The audience loved the show and showed that love with strong applause. They left the stage and returned to their table.

"Wow! They were really good." Victoria said as she and Dove ate and enjoyed the smoked salmon.

"Wait until you see Hawk perform sweetheart," Dove sipped on his soda. "I think he goes on next."

Kenny went back on stage. "Next we have the one and only microphone marauder, he's been blowing up spots all over the D.C. area. He's about to bring it to you, I present to you Hawk!"

Hawk got on stage and took the microphone from the stand. DJ Expression played his DAT. His track began and he performed his song "*The Master Plan*," a song about the year 2001 and the "New World Order." After Hawk finished that song, he received applause from the crowd. Then, a familiar instrumental song drifted through the air that caused Dove to look up from his plate and focus on the stage.

"Come on up on stage partner." Kenny came up from behind and handed Dove a cordless microphone.

"Surprise." Victoria said.

Dove kissed his wife, took off his suit jacket, loosened his tie and walked onto the stage. Hawk and Dove began to freestyle.

DOVE:
Well it's me the Dove
Always shouting one love
Like Marley I'm Barley.

HAWK:
And I'm the oats
Coming like a gang of Redcoats
Verbally attacking on American soil
Slamming like a battle royal.

DOVE:
That's royale, don't mean to correct you,
Hawk, you're my bro you know I respect you.
You know we connect like two plus two.

HAWK:
That's four like the Fantastic
Add one for five like the Furious
Coming through the loudspeakers
Making sure they're hearing us.

When the beat went off Hawk and Dove began to perform *Broken Glass*. As they rhymed Victoria couldn't believe how sexy her husband looked on stage. She was completely turned on.

After they performed Dove hugged Hawk and said. "Thanks man, that was so much fun."

"Just like old times." Hawk said as Dove returned to his table and put his suit jacket back on.

"You really looked good on stage." Victoria said.

"Thank you." Dove said as he sat down and adjusted his tie.

"Do you miss the single life and hanging out with your friends?" She asked.

"I wouldn't trade what I have for anything in the world." Dove said.

"Not even for the fortune that fame brings?" She asked.

"Vicki, with you and Julia I'm the richest man on earth."

"How sweet." She reached over and kissed him and

said. "When we get home you can give me a private performance."

"See that couple over there?" Dove pointed at Culture and Polly.

"Yeah, they look really happy." Victoria said.

"They've been together longer than this place has been open, I want to grow old with you just like that." Dove said.

"No matter what I'll always be here right by your side as your wife." She held his hand. "And that's the truth."

Dana, Paradise, Hawk and Dove sat there and watched them kiss.

"See Mood, love can still be a beautiful thing." Paradise said to Mood.

Mood looked down at his Cajun Chicken Pasta and said. "You know I wrote a special poem to dedicate my love to this woman only to find out she was playing one against the other. I feel like a fool. That's the last time I act on my feelings."

"Hold on Mood," Paradise said. "You should feel lucky, most people go their whole lives not even experiencing love on any level. Just because it didn't work out for you, you're hatin'. Love is hard, she was the one that let a great guy go."

"Yeah Mood, love is a gamble but it's always worth the risk," Dana said. "Hurting the next one is not gonna make you feel any better."

"You know what Mood? It may not seem like it now but you will emerge from this a better person," Hawk said. "I know it would've made me a better person. If you leave this relationship with bitterness in your heart, you'll only take it out on the next person. That makes you selfish and that's not your style man."

Mood heard all that they were saying and said. "You're right, I just wish that it could've ended better."

"Maybe you could call her one day and give it some closure." Eboni said.

Kenny walked onto the stage and introduced Mood.

"I have to go," Mood got up and went to the stage. "My name is Theodore Moody." Mood looked down at the poem he wrote for Sabrina, crumbled it into a ball and dropped it on the floor. He closed his eyes began:

I always used the word love as an excuse to lay a
woman down
And sex as my weapon of choice.
Using the same lines on women time after time,
Laughing inside because I was numb from emotion,
Never experiencing true love, never caring enough to
try.
My mother always told me, I'd know love when I felt
butterflies.
You made me feel those butterflies
The day you walked into my life.
And every time I saw you,
I felt them over and over again,
And I had to see you 'cause I loved that feeling.

When we laid and made love for the first time,
I realized God is the essence of love
Because something this beautiful
Must be heaven sent

Like a caterpillar to a butterfly,
Love transforms something basic
Into something beautiful.

He walked off the stage and received handshakes from the guys and hugs from the ladies as he walked back to the table. "What I'm taking from this experience is the hope that I'll be able to feel that way for another woman. When, not if, but when I do I'll be better at it because I've loved once before." Then he sat down and finished his dinner.

A beautiful brown skin woman approached him. "That

was a beautiful poem, not a lot of brothers can discuss love with such raw emotion."

"You're beautiful, where are you from?" Mood tried to place her accent.

"Jamaica," She said. "My sister and I were wondering if you wanted to sit with us?"

Mood looked at the table her identical twin waved at him.

"Sure," Mood got up. "I'll be over there if you need me." He said to his friends as he walked away with the beautiful brown skin woman.

"It looks like Mood recovered rather quickly." Paradise shook her head.

"I would say so." Dana agreed.

"Daaamn. He could've took me with him." Hawk said.

Kenny came out of the kitchen with two dozen red and white roses and stopped in front of Dana. "These are for you." He was so nervous his voice cracked.

"For me?" Dana was breathless.

"One rose for every hour of the day I think about you."

Everyone stared as Kenny finally poured his heart out to Dana.

"Dana, I want to be the one you call in the middle of the night, the one who takes you to romantic places all over the city, the one who will hold you if you cry. I'm tired of letting you leave here night after night without telling you how I feel."

"It's about time." Dana hugged him.

The whole restaurant applauded. Culture and Polly watched Kenny and said. "It's about time that boy got off his ass and got together with that girl."

"Like father, like son." Polly put her arm around him.

"What's that supposed to mean?" He asked as he watched Kenny hug Dana.

"You were the same way when we first met."

He turned to her and said. "That's cause your father hated me but that's what made me want you more."

166

"Did my father scare you?" Polly asked.

"Yeah, as long as we were together he made it a point to let me know about his shotgun." They laughed.

Kenny heard them and went back to the kitchen and came out with a dozen roses for his mother. "These are for you Mom, I love you." He kissed her on the cheek.

"Thank you son." She said.

"He gets that from me." Culture said.

"There you go co-signing again." She smiled as Culture kissed Polly on the cheek.

"Excuse me please." Scat left the table and got on stage.

"Ladies and gentlemen, thank you for coming out this evening to celebrate 35 years of good food, good jazz and good people. Like a griot this place has got a story to tell. This place has lived through the riots, the Vietnam War and the Persian Gulf War. It has always been involved in feeding the homeless and tending to the needs of the community. Culture, please take a bow."

Culture stood up and the people applauded.

Scat continued "This place has a story to tell. The story begins with two friends who grew up together in the streets of Newark, N.J. The friends were Culture Baker and Ricardo Lee. They met each other in high school and played in a band with Culture on the bass and Ricardo on the guitar. They joined the Navy together and, during one long tour, they met four other sailors who had the same love for jazz music as they did. After the Korean War, these gentlemen were discharged and toured throughout Europe and America as Nomad. While playing a gig in Washington D.C., Culture met a dancer named Polly Lipton and fell head over heels in love with her. They got married and the band settled in D.C. Ricardo Lee went back to Newark and married his high school sweetheart Janet. On one New Years Eve, Culture had a celebration at his home. The members of the band were there and we were having a good time. Ricardo always could drink all of us under a table. Ricardo got drunk and he and

Culture argued over which one of them should lead on a song that they arranged. Ricardo left the party with Janet, who was three months pregnant at the time. He was very upset, we all tried to calm him down, but he was as stubborn as Culture was. Ricardo pulled up to the main highway from a side road. He turned to the left and watched a car turn into the side road. He pulled out into the main road and into the path of a car that was behind a car that was in the turn lane, because of the icy road, the oncoming car couldn't stop in time and hit Ricardo's car on the driver's side. It killed him instantly. Janet slipped into a coma and died a few days later. Culture blamed himself and it affected the band, we felt it wouldn't be right to carry on without Ricardo. The song that they argued over never got recorded. At the funeral, Culture placed the song in Ricardo's coffin and buried it with him. The name of the song was *The Abstract Griot*. A year later, Culture opened up The Abstract Griot and the rest is history. Culture my friend, you have touched a lot of lives and we thank you. To thank you properly, we want to introduce the Abstract Griot to…" Scat pointed to the stairwell as the members of Nomad descended down the stairs one by one. "…Mr. Mojo Jackson on piano." Mojo, dressed in a black suit, met the stage amid applause, sat at the piano and began to belt out melodies." Culture's eyes lit up, he couldn't believe it.

Scat continued. "On trumpet, Mr. Lincoln Davis." Lincoln came downstairs dressed in Kente and with trumpet in hand. He began playing like the old salt that he was.

"On flute and saxophone, Mr. Grover Bullock." Down the stairs came Grover, dressed in a hounds-tooth suit. Ruth came down behind him and sat at the table with Culture. She hugged Polly while Grover began spitting riffs with his alto saxophone.

"My name is Scat Strayer." Scat's gray locks hung over his brown suit as he sat down behind the drums and belted out a rim shot.

Kenny came down with his dad's bass, placed it on

stage and said. "On the bass, my dad Mr. Culture Baker!"

Culture was still speechless. "Surprise honey." Polly said.

The whole place applauded as Culture stood up and walked to the stage, while the rest of Nomad continued to play. He hugged his son and grabbed the bass.

"Thank you." He said overwhelmed, he began to play the bass and connected with the rest of the band.

The Abstract Griot's audience sat in silence and observed Nomad take improvisation to new heights. At first, they were a little shaky but ten minutes later, they played like they had never stopped playing together. After they were done with their set, Culture turned around, hugged all of the band members. and the Abstract Griot erupted in applause. Culture grabbed the microphone. He looked at Kenny, balled his fist and said. "That's for almost making me cry boy, If only Ricardo could see us now." He turned to the band. "Let's see if they can keep up."

Scat yelled. "Count it off Culture."

"One, two, three, four." Culture yelled.

Nomad played their song, *Keep Up*. Scat played the drums hard and each member tried to keep up with him. For the next hour, they played many of their songs and many classics. They ended with Duke Ellington's *Take the A-Train.*

After their performance, the members of Nomad went to the table where Polly and Ruth sat. The aging men laughed and talked about old times. People gathered around the table, took pictures, got autographs, and shook their hands.

Kenny got on stage and said. "If everyone would please join me outside, Dynamite is going to unveil the mural he spent many a day working on."

They all gathered around outside, the gentle summer breeze caressed them.

Dynamite began. "I was nine when I moved here from Puerto Rico. I immediately fell in love with hip-hop. My goal is to master all four elements, emceeing, graf, breakdancing and DJing. So far I've mastered the art of emceeing and graffiti. A lot of people outside of hip-hop still think graffiti is vandalism. The police even tried to arrest me while I worked on this mural, but it was worth it. Kenny, thank you for allowing me to flex my second voice in hip-hop with this mural."

Dynamite lifted the sheet and unveiled the mural and everyone stood there and just stared. The background was a blue sky with two white clouds, above it was an unrolled scroll that read.

"Peace to The Abstract Griots."

On one cloud were the legends of jazz: Ella Fitzgerald, Billie Holiday, Louie Armstrong, Miles Davis, Charles Mingus, Thelonious Monk, Eubie Blake, John Coltrane, Dizzy Gillespe, Sarah Vaughn, and Ricardo Lee. All of these legends were performing together.

On another cloud were the deceased legends of hip-hop: Eazy E, Tupac Shakur, Biggie Smalls, Buffy of the Fat Boys, M.C. Trouble, Trouble T-Roy, Cowboy, DJ Scott La Rock and Filli. They performing together, too.

The legends performed for someone who sat on a throne in the middle. Only three items could be seen from the back of the throne: dreadlocks, a halo and a pair of black hands that reached out to the performers. Everyone stood there among the "oohs" and "aahs."

Paradise took a picture. "Dynamite, this is amazing, what inspired this?"

"My love for the music and for y'all always keeping my third eye open," He looked up at the mural. "All these artists are an inspiration."

Mojo Jackson had his arm around Eboni. "This is incredible, you've captured all the artists in their prime. Did you really do this with spray paint?"

"I sure did sir." Dynamite beamed.

Incredible, I have to take a picture."

Mood looked at the picture and asked. "Who's that emcee who is rhyming on the cloud beside M.C. Trouble?"

"That's an emcee named Filli, he was down with the Amphibians. He had an incredible flow and he always had a smile on his face, he recently died of an asthma attack. Every Thursday night, he held a session at Nayla's that brought out the talented local emcees. He was an inspiration, he rhymed strictly for the love of the music and he was an incredible friend. He will definitely be missed, putting him on this mural is my own personal dedication to him. He deserves to be among the great ones of hip-hop."

Mojo took out his camera and snapped a picture. Then Eboni took the camera from him and said. "Dad, get in front of the mural. Mr. Baker, Mr. Strayer, Mr. Bullock and Mr. Davis, could you please join my father?"

They stood in front of the mural, right beside the image of Ricardo Lee. They locked arms, smiled and posed while Eboni took their picture.

"Come through tomorrow for lunch, It's on me and my son better not charge his old man." Culture caused the small crowd to laugh.

"Yeah, maybe we can get together tomorrow and jam." Scat said.

Victoria looked at her watch. "Lawrence, it's getting late, we'd better be leaving before that boat leaves us."

"You're right baby." Dove said.

Raindance looked up at the sky. "It's beautiful outside, let's go to Georgetown."

"We can walk up M Street and chill out." Flame said.

"That sounds like fun," Hawk said. "Do you want to come with us Eboni?"

"I'd love to," Eboni smiled. "That sounds like fun."

"You coming Mood?" FOG asked.

"No," Mood pointed to the red BMW with the identical twins waiting for him. "I'm afraid I'm going to miss this one."

"I've got to stay and help clean up." Kenny said.

Grabbing his hand Dana said. "I'll stay with you."

"Hold up everybody, before we go our separate ways tonight, let's take a picture." Paradise pulled out her camera.

Kenny, Dana, Mood, Hawk, Eboni, Dove, Victoria, Raindance, Flame, Dynamite, FOG and Paradise all got in front of the mural while Polly Baker took the picture.

"Alright everybody say cheese."

"CHEESE." They all said in unison.

ABOUT THE AUTHOR

As a young child growing up in Brooklyn NY, Troy L. Thompson always dreamed of becoming a writer. Inspired by Langston Hughes, Troy began writing poetry and short stories at an early age. Troy's goal is to embrace all mediums of writing. After serving four years in the United States Marine Corps he moved to Washington D.C. and became a Staff writer for *Straight from the Streets Magazine*; he was also the first archivist for the *Freestyle Union*, a hip-hop collective that started in D.C. and the *Amphibians*. He is currently living and writing in Bowie MD, a suburb of D.C. *The Abstract Griot* is his debut novel.